The Immortals of Lionswood Academy #1

Pawn takes Knight

The Immortals of Lionswood Academy #1

Pawn takes Knight

ELIZABETH STEVENS WRITING AS

E.J. KNOX

Kinky Siren
an imprint of Sleeping Dragon Books

Pawn takes Knight
by E.J. Knox

Print ISBN: 978-1925928365
Digital ISBN: 978-1923017108

Cover art by: Izzie Duffield

Worldwide Electronic & Digital Rights
Worldwide English Language Print Rights

to Word's dictionary,
Where would I be without you worrying
about people being offended by swear words?

Contents

Author Note

This is a dark, angsty, contemporary, boarding school, new adult bully/enemies-to-lovers romance Do not engage in public consumption unless your poker face is impenetrable.

Do not read if you don't like alpha males who'd do anything for their woman, a feisty heroine unafraid of her scars, or fake dating full of passion and dirty words.

This is book one of a novella series, acting as an introduction to the world and inciting the main story arc. While this book ends with a resolution, it is only step one in Raine's revenge. This story will continue in *Knight takes Bishop*, and does not conclude until book five.

It contains themes and scenes that might be distressing to some readers, including mentions of self-harm and rape (occurring off-page), as well as instances of suicidal thoughts, sexual scenes, and physical/emotional violence.

While set in a non-descript part of Europe, this book is written using Australian English because the author is Australian. This will affect the spelling, grammar and syntax you may be used to. It might come across as typos, awkward sentences, poor grammar, or missed/wrong words. In the majority of cases (I won't claim it's infallible, despite all best efforts), this is intentional. I still hope you enjoy it, though!

Chapter One

My heart beat ragged in my chest. I heard it. I felt it. It spelled out words. Words that beat in my skull.

Fear.

Pain.

Danger.

...Run.

Always. Run.

With every blink, the scene unfolds behind my eyes like flashing light illuminating the beast of my nightmares as it stalks closer. I'm drowning. Always drowning. Fighting for breath. One face. Then another. Sneers. Jabs.

"That's what you get for disobeying."

More light. A phoenix to lift me up and out to safety.

But I'm not safe. I'm never safe.

My heart beat harder.

Anger.

Pain.

...Fight.

As I breathed deeply, desperate to return my heart to its usual rhythm, it only beat out one word. Over and over. I'd vowed it would be the last word my heart ever beat.

Revenge.

The word had fuelled my existence for the past ten months.

It made waking up in cold sweats bearable.

It gave me the strength to stop the fear and pain overwhelm me completely.

It was the drive I needed to make it to another day.

Those who had wronged me would pay if it was the last thing I did. My life was a small price to pay for vengeance. If I was going down, I was taking them all with me.

"Raine?" I heard from beside me and it pulled me from the endless circling of my mind.

"Hmm?" I replied, still looking out the Pullman Guard's window.

"It's not too late, you know," Mum said. Her voice was quiet. Hesitant. It was always quiet. Hesitant.

I didn't know if there was any love between my parents. I did know that wasn't the point. Their relationship wasn't one of lovers. They weren't even peers. It was transactional. More money. Heirs. Strength. Dad didn't treat her poorly – that I knew of – but he didn't require her opinions on anything. She spoke only when spoken to. The only exception was me. She'd have stormed the gates of Hell for me if she knew that would help. Sadly, the thought hadn't even occurred to her.

"I need to do this," I told her firmly.

I caught my dad's eye from his seat across from us. His jaw was tight, his eyes were hard, but he gave a simple nod. It was his equivalent of a high five or a hug.

Subconsciously, I hugged my shoulder bag closer on my lap. Dad noted the motion.

"You have it?" he asked, his eyes rising back to mine.

I nodded, my hand gripping the bottom of the bag like a lifeline. "I have it."

One more simple nod. "Do not lose it."

My hand loosened from my bag like I was worried that I'd

cause damage if I held on too tightly. Which was ridiculous because there was nothing I could do to break with my own hands the tactical pocket knife my dad had given me when I'd convinced him to let me do this.

I returned his simple nod and we both looked out our respective windows.

The rest of the trip was passed in silence. Deafening silence.

I could feel the uncertainty and fear radiating off my mother. I could feel the pride and the wrath emanating from my father. Neither of them had ever doubted my story. They had, though, disagreed about how to handle it.

After what felt like hours, the Pullman pulled up in front of the administration building. I got out and looked over the familiar grounds. Quads and lawns dotted with soaring gothic stone buildings, interspersed with winding mazes and surrounded by lush forest. Lionswood Academy hadn't changed for my absence.

Trepidation crawled over my skin, clinging to my back and making me second guess my choices. But I would not be bowed by fear. I hadn't spent the past ten months building a thicker skin – building an impenetrable armour – to let fear put me from my path now.

The students, already in their maroon and navy uniforms, paid us no more mind than any other new student walking into the administration building. They didn't recognise me. And well they shouldn't.

"Sir Edwards. Mrs Edwards," the Dean said, already waiting for us in Reception.

Dean Granville's eyes fell on me, and I saw them widen in surprise. His mouth pressed together like he had to stop himself exclaiming something inappropriate. Then he blinked quickly and covered with a forced smile. It was the same reaction I'd got from anyone who'd looked at me in the past ten months.

I angled my head, so my hair hung further over my face. More for his comfort than mine.

"Raine," he said. "It's good to see you."

We followed him into his office and sat down.

"What can I do for you?" the Dean asked, as though he didn't know why we were there.

"We'd like to re-enrol Raine," my father answered.

The Dean blinked, but kept his surprise to himself. Had he really thought we were here for something else? And what? A law suit? Pfft. "We'd be happy to have her."

"But she is to be kept under the radar. No announcements. No drawing attention to her. She's treated like any random student lucky enough to win a scholarship."

"Raine is hardly a random student lucky enough to win a scholarship," the Dean scoffed, his eyes sliding off Dad, then straight back there after he accidentally looked at my face.

"No," my father agreed, his tone full of everything that didn't need to be said. "Yet she is to be treated as such."

"This is highly irregular," the Dean pointed out.

Despite my parents' reservations, my dad held his own. "A lot goes on in this school that is highly irregular, Damian. Families like ours, the Porters, Wolfes, Lanes, the…Flintlocks. We pay to allow the highly irregular."

Dad looked at me and I felt a small surge of pride at the lengths we'd come these last few months. A year ago, my father had barely looked at me at all. Now, when he did, I saw a growing respect. Mum may not have agreed with my plan and Dad might not be sure I could pull it off, but at least he was going to help me as much as he was able. By help, I of course meant support. The job was all mine. And, who knew. If I did pull it off, maybe I'd finally be the heir he wanted. That would be an unexpected, but not wholly unpleasant side effect.

"You let their children get up to all manner of things in the dark," Dad continued, his tone firm and commanding. "All we're asking is that you don't point out that Raine has returned."

The Dean looked uncertain for a moment.

"Need I remind you that nothing was done to punish West Flintlock and his friends?" Dad pushed, a threat noticeable in his voice.

The Dean seemed to get back some of his nerve. Some. "There was no evidence."

Exactly why we hadn't been to the authorities. That, and my father wasn't exactly a 'go to the authorities' kind of guy. The things you were allowed to know after your parents realised that maybe the good little princess they'd groomed you to be had been extinguished.

Dad inclined his head and leant towards the Dean, another threat. "None but my daughter's face."

The Dean avoided looking at said face at that very moment, though his head twitched like it cost an effort. "You know the school's policy. If it's not a school matter, then it's between the families involved."

"Oh, believe me," Dad said smoothly, a humourless smirk tugging at the corner of his lips. "We'll be taking matters into our own hands."

Then he looked at me sternly. We'd had this talk. If I failed, he stepped in. The merger West and I would have brought between the Edwards and Flintlock families would have been a boon. That being said, after what happened, my father was more than happy to stomp the Flintlocks into the ground – six foot deep, if necessary – as soon as I gave the word. As soon as I failed.

To say I'd had an education over the last year as to the deeper nature of my world and our families would be a severe understatement. I knew, though, that there was plenty more I still had to learn.

The Dean nodded resignedly. "We just ask you keep all dead bodies off school grounds." By the way he said it, it was obviously a policy he had to remind people of often. That didn't surprise me.

The Dean and Dad looked to me.

I couldn't guarantee that West would survive my retribution. All going to plan, there'd be nothing left of him but a name on the Foxfield Hall Order of Service. But I could do my best to do it off campus.

I nodded. "Fine."

The Dean was all smiles again, even if it didn't quite reach his eyes. "Brilliant. Welcome back, Raine. It's lovely to have you at Lionswood Academy once again. We will downplay your presence as much as practicable until you so wish otherwise." He looked to my father. "Satisfactory?"

Dad nodded. "Very. Pleasure doing business with you, Damian."

Both men stood and the Dean took Dad's outstretched hand with a nod of his own.

"Anything for an alum," Dean Granville said, far more meaning to his words than they alone conveyed.

Because that was how our world worked. Connections. With them, you ruled the world. Without them, you were nothing. Nobody. Stepped on by every other person. Lionswood was an institution. Our parents' parents' parents' parents had gone to Lionswood. Going back generations. Each one grew up privileged and entitled. They grew up to raise the next generation of privilege and entitlement. And on it went. Everyone had a place. Those places were respected.

And the Edwards family was among the most respected. At least, we had been in Dad's generation. Suffering the tragic and unlucky condition of being born female, I'd automatically lost a lot of the clout Dad had spent his school years growing to ridiculous proportions. But not for long. I was going to put the name of Edwards back on top, even if it killed me as well.

My parents weren't ones for unnecessary affection. After organising the necessary payment and enrolment details, they left. Our goodbye was brief, then I was lugging my bags to my room and their Pullman was gliding off down the driveway again and wouldn't be seen again until at least the Christmas holidays, if even then.

I opened the door to my room and looked around. Very different to the one I'd left vacant the year before in the Manor, it was basic. They all were, until they were lived in, and my previous room had been lived in for over three years. Twin bed and bedside by one wall. More cell than window in the two-metre-thick outer wall, covered with a thick velvet curtain to aid in keeping the chill winter winds out. Tiny hearth on the wall across from the bed, tended in the cooler months by an army of servants employed for that exact purpose. A chest of draws and wardrobe next to the door, and a trunk at the end of the bed. Lastly, a small desk with one of the least comfortable chairs imaginable. That I remembered. I already had a new one on the way.

It wasn't a huge school – maybe three hundred students – so it was easy for the students to have their own rooms. It was supposed to foster independent study and good sleeping habits. All it did was give people a little extra privacy – or not, depending on what you liked – for their extracurricular shenanigans.

Those extracurricular shenanigans had always been something I heard about – I knew about – but never thought applied to me. It was for people like the Immortals. The ones with no morals or code. The bad ones. The naughty ones. The depraved ones. The ones who got into trouble and who the Elites looked down on.

Looking back, I saw how ridiculously sheltered and immature I'd been kept. I'd been naïve and that had been my downfall. No student at Lionswood was innocent. They all came from families just the same as the Immortals. The only difference between the Elites and the Immortals was that the Immortals didn't hide who they really were behind an upper-class façade as though their money and lifestyle was always on the up and up.

And that included my family.

As an Elite, I'd been all fairy tales and romances. Pretty dinners and ballgowns. I'd been distracted from the darker aspects by shiny things and flattery. And those around me had taken pains to keep me that way.

After last year, the rose-coloured glasses were gone, and I saw this world for what it was. Use or be used. They'd tried to use me. It was my turn to use them.

I hadn't had a plan beyond returning to Lionswood. As I went through the achingly familiar ritual of getting settled in my dorm room, I tried to formulate one. Aside from wanting revenge, and spending the previous ten months toughening myself up to get it, I didn't know the *how* of it. I could see my goal, but the road to get there was a gaping chasm I didn't know how to even begin to cross. But I was a smart girl. Surely, I'd find a way. All I had to do was really put my mind to it.

However, after an hour or so, I was unpacked and unsettled in my room, and I still didn't know how I was going to eek out my vengeance. But I wouldn't let that get me down.

I headed out into the school, hunching into my blazer. Once on school grounds, it was proper to be in uniform Monday to Friday between eight in the morning and six in the evening, unless you were unfortunate enough to be stuck on campus during the holidays. And it was Monday, the day before the term properly started, and only three in the afternoon.

By now, more students had arrived and were greeting each other with the enthusiasm of friends who hadn't seen each other for months. I recognised almost all of them, even the ones who'd started last year when I'd only been around for two months. My brain was good like that. I never forgot a face.

Never.

Except one.

Every time I tried to picture it, all I could remember – all I saw – was that rising phoenix. Like some cruel joke, urging me to rise from the ashes of my pain, it seemed burned into my memory in place of any face.

Just the thought of it had the power to make me highly agitated – my heart raced, my breath grew short and shallow, my palms got sweaty, and I wanted to run – and yet somehow also calmed me. Calmed my mind. That phoenix snuck a spark of something bright into the darkness that had consumed me. The darkness that filled me up until there was nothing left but hate and anger and weakness that I was determined to fight.

My soul was black. Black as pitch. Expect when that fucking spark burnt in the corner of my eye. I'd held onto it – to the black – through all the darkest parts of my healing. Many of which I was still fighting my way through.

As I rounded the outer wall of the dormitory in the direction of Foxfield Hall, on my way no where particular, I heard a familiar laugh that cut right through me and made me freeze. My heart thudded and fluttered in the very opposite of harmony. My mind went blank. My mouth went dry. My body shook and vibrated in fear.

The laugh was so loud and carefree. After all, what did he have to worry about? The world worshipped at his feet. And, from those who didn't worship, he was protected.

I stared, dumbfounded, as he walked towards me.

No thoughts.

Unable to move.

I was back in that day. The day everything changed.

His gaze lifted and he looked right at me.

My heart stopped in my chest, but not the way it used to when he looked at me. Where once I felt hope and love, there was just dread and an echoed recollection of lust for payback that I couldn't quite keep hold of in that moment.

His eyes stayed on me for the space of one painfully slow heartbeat. Two. But finally, he looked away without the faintest glimmer of recognition for the girl behind the dark brown hair.

If I wanted any chance of taking him off-guard, he couldn't know I was back. The only way I thought I could keep a low profile was if my outsides changed as much as my insides. Before seeing West, I hadn't been sure that I'd done enough. But his reaction – or lack of – told me step one was complete. There was nothing left of the girl he'd known anymore.

West Flintlock, though, hadn't changed in my absence. Not really. He'd filled out a bit, lost some of that roundness of childhood. The beautiful boy was turning into the breathtaking man he'd always threatened to become. It was enough for me to almost forget myself for a split-second as he smirked at something one of his court said. He was a stunning specimen of confidence, authority, and glamour. But I saw through him now.

Dark blond hair swept up and back from his face. Nearly six feet tall. Deep blue eyes like a starry night sky. He carried himself with even more untouchable arrogance than the year before when we'd walked around the campus, his arm draped around *my* shoulder just the way his arm now draped around *her* shoulder.

The usurper to my crown, to my boyfriend, to my life. As far as I was concerned, the shitty little backstabber could keep him. But I'd see how much she wanted what was left of him after I was done with him.

I'd spent ten months preparing for this. I'd trained for this.

West Flintlock had better lock his doors because I was coming for him.

Chapter Two

Friday morning was the earliest I dared leaving my dorm before chapel and, by the time I'd built up the courage, I was chomping at the bit. Until then, I'd been cooped up in my own four walls, not daring to leave more than necessary and risk discovery. And certainly not for something so noticeable as a run.

I got changed into my running gear and did my usual first-thing exercise to serve as a warmup.

It hadn't been enough to just toughen my mind these past few months. To force it to function even while I was in the throes of memory. Even with all the work I'd put in, with psychiatrists and psychologists and my own private regimen that none of my psychs would have condoned, I'd still frozen every time I saw West that week.

Every time there was a possibility that I'd be found alone with an Elite.

At the beginning of a lesson or the end of a lesson.

Sequestered in a darkened corner of the library.

In the line for meals in the dining hall.

None of them had recognised me, even in the girl's bathroom, but it hadn't stopped the fear being stronger than I'd expected.

So, I had to keep my body strong, too. Crunches. Weights. Running. Boxing. I'd taken it all up in the last ten months. At first, I'd hated it, but I'd forced myself to do a little each day until it was habit, until I got antsy if I went a day without it. And I'd gone for a week without a morning run.

As I warmed up, I visualised everything. It kept me focussed and motivated me. I relived every hit, every kick, every nail digging into my skin, every drop of blood I'd shed, every promised threat. My cheek on fire. My arms and legs held down. My skirt pushed up. Hands at my pants. Fighting. Always fighting. No use.

Fear.

Pain.

Danger.

...Run.

But I'd survived, even if I wasn't sure how. All I could remember was one minute I was sure I was dead, the next all I could picture was that stupid phoenix, then I was waking up in the hospital. I'd survived the worst they'd tried on me. Changed and determined.

Anger.

Pain.

...Fight.

Primed and ready, I slipped out of my room and out into the cool September morning air. The sun was barely peeking over the horizon. No one was around. I had the school grounds to myself, but I still didn't want to risk running into anyone else. Without a crowd to disappear into, who knew who might see me and recognise me with my hair up and out of my way, great, whopping scar or not.

There was a track through the woods that the cross-country team trained on. Why a place like Lionswood had a cross country team, I didn't know. I was sure now that it had other uses; like survival skills training or How to Dispose of a Dead

Body 101.

A year ago, the track would have kicked my arse. Between inclines and roots and rocks, I would have been on my face not even three steps in. But I'd been loath to venture too far from home recently, and we'd only had very similar conditions for me to run in. Even so, I was breathing deeply and sweat sheened my skin after not too long. In the comfort of the woods, the air was still cool against my skin and the chill spurned me on.

Out here, I was free from it all. I left my problems behind and only focussed on one foot in front of the other, the steady, reassuring beat of my heart in my chest, my breath on the air. Out here, I wasn't Raine Edwards – victim – I was just Raine. A version of myself I could have been in a very different world.

I pulled my hair from the tie, making sure it was loose and draped over my face before I left the woods. Which was lucky because, even though it was still only eight o'clock, students were up and about. No one looked at me twice; I wasn't the only runner at Lionswood, I just might have been the earliest riser.

Moving from class to class during the week had afforded some anonymity. Students had been more concerned with what their friends were up to, how ready they were for their teachers, and hazing the new Year Eights than they were with random kids who kept to themselves. And that morning was no exception.

Shower. Changed into uniform. Off to class.

Without a hitch.

I got through the whole morning and my status continued unchanged.

Safe.

Running was back on the schedule.

The amount I ate had fallen drastically the year before. I just didn't get hungry the way I used to. Not for food. I had to purposefully force myself to remember to eat and, knowing I'd missed breakfast, I made sure to be at lunch. I went early in the hopes that I could avoid the main rush, but I found myself lingering at my seat as I watched the people around me go about their lives.

The loser table in the dining hall hadn't changed in my absence. It was still the table closest to the kitchen doors. It was still populated by kids who talked as little – or less – to each other than to their bullies.

It was a symbol of their ostracism. Putting them as physically outside the cliques of Lionswood Academy as they were socially.

But it suited me fine.

And gave me a perfect vantage of the Elite's table in the middle of the room. Of every table actually.

First night back, I'd claimed the seat closest to the corner of the room, my back to two walls. From there, I could see them all.

Yakuza.

Irish Mob.

Camorra.

Plutonis Satellites.

Sicilian Mafia.

Russians.

Triads.

Dominicans.

The kids of the worst of the worst. They went through one of the vast networks of schools of which Lionswood Academy was a proud part before being unleashed on the unsuspecting world.

Even when I was young and naive – stupid, more like – I knew our world was different. It wasn't like the world you saw on TV or in movies. It just didn't work like that. Life wasn't all school, friends, the mall, Netflix. We had a deeper layer to everything, a strict approved parameter of behaviour depending on who we were talking to and who they were affiliated with. The wrong word – the wrong action – around the wrong person, and the consequences were more than just the moral code that ran the rest of the world.

Everything was blood.

Payment was made in blood as often as your preferred currency. Warnings were given in blood. Threats carried out in blood. Alliances sealed in blood.

Fuck love.

Blood makes this world go around.

Even for people like the Elites, and certainly for people like the Immortals.

Lionswood was ruled by two branches of hierarchy, affectionately known as the CEOs and the Crims, but both more dangerous than either moniker suggested. It had been that way for longer than my remembered ancestors and would be that way until long after any of us were forgotten.

The Elites.

The Immortals.

The Elites were the children of the shady and corrupt riches of the world. CEOs. Peers of their respective realms. Law enforcement. Those who fronted legitimate business to the world but stacked their pockets with less than legal enterprises. At the top of their hierarchy was the King of Lionswood Academy. Currently atop that lofty throne was West Flintlock, the boy who would get away with everything. He'd won the position after the incident of the year before; the first Year

Eleven to unseat a Year Thirteen in over a hundred years. Everyone looked up to the Elites or feared them.

Everyone but the Immortals. The children of those who didn't need or want legitimate business to be their façade. Assassins. Weapons runners. Drug cartels. They lived in the shadows and reigned there with an iron fist. At Lionswood, they were ruled over by the Lord of Lionswood Academy, and Dante Wolfe couldn't give any less shits about West than he already did. West was less than a bug on the sole of his very big boots. Dante had been the Lord since he stepped foot on school grounds at the tender age of thirteen. Our very first day at Lionswood Academy, Dante had challenged the sitting Lord and beaten him so badly he'd been off campus for a month. Dante had taken his place with no contestation from the establishment and full support from the rest of the Immortals.

I watched the Elites at their table in the very middle of the dining hall, pride of place, a symbol of their power and status. Like everything else around me, their table hadn't changed while I'd been away. West sat in the middle of the table with his girlfriend on his left – the position I had once held – and his lieutenant on his right. The sight of Fletcher Porter made my skin crawl and my heart thud painfully in my chest.

Fear.

Pain.

Danger.

...Run.

I forced myself to take a deep breath.

Anger.

Pain.

...Fight.

I wouldn't let Fletch have any hold on me anymore. He'd pay for the part he played in my downfall. He may not have physically touched me, but he'd done enough. Or, rather, he'd stood by and done nothing. Which was just as bad. I would never forgive him, even after everything we'd been through.

Revenge.

A great burst of jeering laughter came from the opposite corner of the room, from the Immortals table, and pulled my attention.

Dante was standing next to his table with a kid half his size in front of him. I couldn't hear what was said over the hubbub through the rest of the hall. Bullying was commonplace – nay, encouraged – within the hallowed grounds of Lionswood. No one paid them any more interest than a passing glance in case it was relevant or particularly vicious. It wasn't either of those things.

No doubt that small kid had just done something innocuously stupid like bump Dante with an elbow or knock something off his tray onto the Lord of the Immortals. He looked like a Year Eight, and a tiny one at that. He barely reached Dante's chest, a chest I was sure was bigger than it had been the year earlier.

As I watched the standoff on the other side of the hall, Dante took a step towards the kid and the kid didn't take a step back quickly enough. The simplest of nudges from Dante was enough to send him sprawling onto his arse behind him, his tray of food falling all over his head and his lap as laughter echoed around the hall from those who'd watched the spectacle.

That was how Dante operated. The least amount of effort required. Whether that was pounding a guy into the pavement, or a stern frown from across the room. And it worked. Everyone just let it work. He didn't raise his fists to those far smaller than him, not unless they directly challenged him. But then, I'd learned the Immortals had a code, as immoral and self-serving as it was, that the Elites for all their act of superior refinement lacked.

Dante's bored eyes roved the hall as he waited for the kid to get to shaking feet. They alighted on me for a second longer than they should have, and my heart thudded. Nothing passed over his face, so I was fairly sure he hadn't recognised me either. And why would he? He'd barely looked at me when my skin was porcelain perfection and blemish free thanks to a shit tonne of makeup, and my hair was bouncing blonde curls. He wasn't going to recognise me with a great ugly scar burrowed into my au naturel cheek and loose, dark brown hair hanging over my face.

I looked back to the Elites. At her. Talulla Buckingham. West had styled her in perfect imitation of the girl I used to be. Dark blonde hair with lighter highlights, pulled back into an elegant bun with curled wisps meticulously placed to look like they were escaping, carefree, to frame her face. She wore her uniform with absolute perfection, tailored to fit her body as snugly as possible. Her white school shirt, clinging navy jumper, fitted maroon blazer, striped tie, navy and maroon checked skirt reaching her mid-thigh, tall white socks that almost met her skirt, and black mary-janes like any other school shoe but with a noticeably taller heel. She was me just a year ago.

I wondered how she felt about it. Did she see me every time she looked in the mirror? Or was she too obsessed with West to care he had a type, and her previous look wasn't it. She'd definitely fought hard enough to usurp my place; it wasn't that big a leap to assume she wanted West at any cost. Even if that cost was to become me.

I certainly didn't see me when I looked in the mirror

anymore. The only person who looked back at me was tired. She had the pallor of the sick. Limp dark hair hung over at least half my face at all times, usually leaving my scar on show. I'd stopped wearing my contacts and switched to glasses with dark brown frames. No one from my life before would think of Raine Edwards and think scarred, dark, and glasses. It was the perfect disguise, short of wearing a mask, but that would have just drawn more questions.

In the dining hall of Lionswood Academy, every table – every affiliation – had its own dynamic. Its own rules and hierarchy. And the Elites were the only ones who treated each other as poorly as they treated everyone else. I hadn't thought anything of it until the year before. Now I saw them for what they were, but I guessed that's what happened when you made up a clique of people who came from families used to being above everyone else in their life.

Fletch poured chocolate milk onto Caesar's head. Despite the lengths Talulla had gone to in order to steal West from me, Zina was shoving her chest into West's face, and he was welcoming her with open arms. Matteo slapped Guillermo upside the head for nothing more than sitting next to him. Steffi and Rochelle started a fight over Christophe, who had his tongue down Arabella's throat. And West just laughed it all off.

They were petty and shallow and so pathetic. Each of them vying for their King's approval. The shittier they were to each other, the more he approved. Watching them from the outside, I had to wonder if it was a ploy. The Elites couldn't band together and overthrow West if they didn't trust each other.

It was a stark reminder that I used to be that petty and shallow and pathetic. Like every single Elite at that table, I'd been nothing but a pawn of the King. West had placed us and played us perfectly to keep hold of his power.

He'd fucked up when he'd discarded me.

I was out, and this lowly pawn was going to see to it that the King toppled.

But I still didn't know how I was going to achieve that.

I could try to seduce West back to me. Lull him into a sense of complacency. Play the dutiful and loyal girlfriend. Then gut him in his sleep. The idea appealed. Turn on him what he did to me; play perfect then rip off the mask and reveal the ugliness beneath.

The problem with that plan was that just the idea of it, while appealing, made my hand shake so hard I had to fist it and put it on my leg under the table. The idea of West touching me. Even after everything I'd done to condition myself in the last ten months. Even if it meant seeing myself avenged. Just thinking about him touching me made bile rise and made my heart beat too hard and too fast. It fluttered in my chest, but not in a good way. My heart hadn't fluttered in a good way in…about ten months.

I could just go up and stick my knife in him. The knife I'd hidden in my room for fear that I'd either do exactly that, or someone would take it off me and use it on me. Just killing him would be satisfying. I had no doubt that I could get close enough to him to do it. I'd learnt all the best places to stick my blade, and I was sure I could do some very permanent damage before anyone could stop me.

But what if I missed? What if someone stopped me? What if someone got him help too soon? And, worse, what if someone killed me before I could confirm West was dead? What if I'd kept myself afloat enough to get my revenge these last ten months only to die not knowing if I succeeded?

Fuck.

Neither of those plans would work. Not now anyway. Not yet. Maybe I could find a way to make them work. Eventually. But there were too many variables now.

A start was just being in the same room as him without a full-blown panic attack. I was going to take the win. It showed that everything I'd been through wasn't totally in vain. It showed there was hope. Hope that, even if I didn't have the answers now, that didn't mean I wouldn't be able to find them.

I'd just have to relearn his routine. Discover those weaknesses I'd been too preoccupied to notice before. Use what I did remember, what I did know, and put the pieces together and hope it revealed a way I could use it against him.

West walked past me with Fletch, Jaz and Olivia. My stomach crawled and the very little lunch I'd managed to force down tried making a reappearance. But, even if they felt my eyes drilling holes into them, they didn't seem to notice as the strolled out, West acting the King the Elites had made him.

Something niggled unnervingly at the back of my neck but, when I turned, I didn't see anyone watching me.

Chapter Three

The next week, I still had no ideas on how I could make West pay, but I was also still just some random kid no one bothered with; I was unaffiliated, so bullying me held no interest or benefit to anyone.

Yet.

There would come a point where someone would make a move on me. Someone would get bored of waiting for me to be relevant and decide to see if I was interesting. But there was a whole year level of new, smaller students to get bored of before they'd get to me.

West went about his charmed life like I didn't exist. Which suited me fine. The more people who didn't know I existed, the better.

It was painfully clear to me that I was still very much West's pawn, and it was going to take me more time than I wanted to be able to put into practise everything I'd been training myself to be.

This was his domain. Their domain. They were many and I was one. If I showed my hand too soon then I'd end up worse than before with no revenge to show for it. As much as I wanted to go up to him and sink my knife in his belly every time I saw him, I knew I had to bide my time. Killing West wasn't enough. I needed to ruin him. I might still kill him after – if he didn't do it himself – but I wanted him broken and decimated under my foot before I did.

So that knife was going to have to wait.

As per my father's agreement with the Dean, teachers didn't call on me to answer questions. They acted like the dark-haired shadow at the back of the room wasn't even there. And the students followed suit. With plenty of others being brought to their attention, they were thinking about someone else before they'd had a chance to wonder about me.

So, I could go about my life, feeling a kind of safety that I'd never actually experienced at Lionswood Academy. And I'd certainly never enjoyed that level of anonymity. Not that I'd minded having everyone's eyes on me a year earlier. Oh, how naïve I'd been.

I passed through Foxfield Hall during lunch the next Tuesday. It was a massive building, more mausoleum than anything else. It was where we had all our non-religious assemblies and services. Being not set up for anything currently, the floor was bare. There were a few steps of wooden bleachers at one end of the room, but they barely catered to a quarter of the school. When they had to fit us all in, they set out chairs.

My shoes echoed on the parquetry as I walked around, the sheer magnitude of everything it was gave me an unexpected sense of peace.

The Hall had always been my preference – I'd never been overly religious, and the monks had always unnerved me – but it seemed fitting now, somehow. Like a part of me belonged, to be engraved up on the Order of Service with the rest of the dead.

I looked up at those great marble blocks on the walls and breathed deeply. Reverently.

The Order of Service was a list of all those students who

had died while enrolled at Lionswood Academy. It was split into two sections. The Confirmation List was for those whose death had been claimed as a hit. While the Communion List was reserved for those who had just disappeared, never to be seen or heard from again.

I recognised names on both lists. Not just the family names, but I'd gone to school with a number of them. The Confirmation List was, by far, longer. Both lists had names added as recently as months earlier, and both lists went as far back as five-hundred years. The Lists spanned nearly three-quarters of the two longest walls of the Hall. I had to wonder if any other school in the world had such an impressive and daunting list adorning any of the walls in their buildings.

As I headed back to the Salisbury girls' dormitory hall for my next set of books, my walk took me between buildings. I felt the hairs on the back of my neck really prickle for the first time since I'd been back.

Danger.

Instantly, I looked up and found the Lord of the Immortals facing my direction.

He was far enough away that I couldn't be sure that his eyes were on me, but the instincts curling in my stomach said he was. Only was that coincidence or…? Had he recognised me? Was he watching me, knowing it was me?

And what was he saying to his bishop?

If Dante was a honed missile, Riker Lane was a blunt weapon. A brute. His only job was all muscle. His hair was almost as dark as Dante's, but short on top, with a designed fade at the back and sides. He was more heavily tattooed than Dante and didn't care what the establishment thought of that – luckily it was so commonplace, the establishment didn't much care. The rumours said that no Immortal got where they were without making their first kill at twelve; it was kill or be killed. They also said that Riker's kill count was higher than any Immortal in history, and it was believable. It wasn't just said but known that he'd sworn to kill any Elite. Thankfully for us – or *them*, now – he wasn't allowed to do it on campus.

Though, I was surprised he actually paid attention to what he was and wasn't allowed to do. Riker was the kind of guy to throw his intimidating stature around just to watch, with pure glee, the way the mortals fled in terror. Even West had been known to walk a little faster when Riker gnashed his teeth at him. But then, after Riker had killed one of those very Elites last year before school started, proudly ensuring their name was carved into the Confirmation List, I'd say there was very definite reason to fear him. The only person who'd been able to keep some leash on Riker was Dante, and I wondered what the Lord of the Immortals had done to elicit such loyalty and blind obedience from the good little guard dog.

From the outside, it seemed Riker acted as both henchman and advisor to his Lord. It was well known that, if you wanted an audience with the Lord – be it business or pleasure – you had to go through the Bishop. Though, I doubted that Riker had earned the moniker for his deeply religious principles. They were at mass every Sunday like the good little boys surely not even their grandmothers thought they were, but they didn't exactly strive for a religious life.

Whatever the subject of Riker and Dante's conversation at that moment, Riker didn't turn and look at me as though I was that subject. And it was all of a few tense heartbeats until Dante casually turned and looked away as though there had been nothing remarkable about the direction he'd been looking.

Maybe his eyes on me had just been a coincidence.

I had done everything I could to be unremarkable since my

return. If Dante hadn't looked at me once when looking at me had been the goal, then he wasn't going to notice me now.

And if I reminded myself enough, I might believe it.

But somehow, I couldn't.

I spent the next few days once more lacking that sense of safety, my heart constantly pounding at the idea I might be discovered, who might discover me, and what they'd do to me when they did. I wasn't ready for the only card I held to be discarded quite so early, and without another waiting to back me up.

I'd been a Princess of the Elites. Everyone else hated me.

West had discarded me and ruined me. Whatever they'd been told had happened between us, the Elites hated me.

Nowhere and no one was safe.

And I kept an eye on Dante Wolfe. I had to be ready. If he had recognised me, then it was only a matter of time before he proved it to me. I imagined that him putting it off was simply to make sure I was at my most paranoid and anxious by the time he actually put me out of my misery. I wasn't going to be able to hold my own against Dante physically if he chose to go that route, but I could still put up a pretty decent fight.

I kept an equal eye on West. So far, all the Elites' heads had been shoved so far up West's arse that they hadn't even considered I might have returned. There was something to be said for their simpering, sycophantic fawning; I'd stop completely denigrating anything that helped my cause.

By the middle of the second week of school, both the Immortals and the Elites had got back into the routine of belittlement, bullying, intimidating and disfiguring as many of the other students as possible.

On Wednesday as I headed for the Dupuy Conservatorium of Music, one of the Elite harem, Olivia, was busy taunting some helpless kid in about Year Nine. The poor kid dared to be looking at West with something close to resembling puppy dog eyes and it was Olivia's job to put her in her place for daring to think of him at all.

Back when it had been me at West's side, I'd never been wholly comfortable with the way the Elites teased girls for crushing – or even considering crushing – on West, but I'd felt like it was more that they were protecting my relationship with my man. He was a one-woman man and that was the end of it, no point looking at him because he wasn't on offer.

Good God, but how ten months changed a perspective. West hadn't just stolen my innocence or my face, but he'd stolen all positivity I'd had. I watched everything and everyone with cynicism and distrust now.

That kid who was getting taunted by Olivia was no doubt going to be taken to West's room later that night and shown exactly what she'd get for daring to look at him twice. She'd be given exactly what she probably wasn't even thinking off. And the more she struggled, the more West would probably enjoy it.

I'd feel bad for her, but I was already drowning under the weight of my own shit. I couldn't take on the shit of every single girl West had ruined, or I'd be so leaden that I'd take the whole world with me when I finally sank. I could only hope that West's coming retribution would be enough for all of us. It would be a somewhat hollow victory, but I'd take whatever victory I could get.

In another part of the school, there was a showdown occurring between the Triads and the Irish Mob. In theory, they both had vague ties to the Immortals. Everyone who wasn't an Elite did. But it didn't stop the different affiliations scrapping amongst each other. The Immortals proper were the Lord and his crew, whoever he chose to surround himself with but usually from his own affiliation. It didn't mean that he didn't exercise his authority over the others anyway. Or rather, that his Bishop didn't exercise the Lord's authority over them.

As I passed, Riker was stalking towards the scrap like a man intent on death. He flipped his switchblade open expertly and he walked towards Dáire O'Dooley and Tai 'King' Kong, and they both took more than a few hurried steps away from Riker's oncoming stalk.

With an amused smirk on his face, Dante barked something in Italian at Riker and, after two more steps on Riker's part, he finally stopped and looked back at him. He snapped something in return Italian and Dante shook his head. Riker said something more urgently and Dante said what I recognised as, 'no.' Riker seemed annoyed, but simply shrugged.

"Keep it for those who deserve it," Riker snarled at Dáire and King, who both nodded, glared at each other, then took their crews on their respective ways.

As Riker returned to Dante, I saw Vanda was at Dante's side. She was often found at Dante's side, and I don't think anyone really knew what the Russian was doing with the Italian. They preferred each other over Elites, for sure, but I wasn't sure what the draw between the two of them was. I had to assume it was sexual. So much of the currency at Lionswood was sex.

Blood and sex.

Not always separate.

But they had nothing to do with my revenge scheme, so ultimately I didn't care what Dante and Vanda were to each other. They could fuck each other senseless multiple times a day for all I cared. Unless it had to do with me destroying West, I didn't have time to give mental real estate to it so I just continued on my way and kept vigilant for anything that might disrupt my plans.

By Friday, I was highly strung and just waiting to be ambushed by Dante or West, burrowing into myself and trying to keep inconspicuous as I went about my life. West still didn't seem likely, but I couldn't tell myself anymore that Dante was just a coincidence. Dante was to be considered a threat until further notice, even if I didn't have a shred of proof that he'd recognised me.

On my way to the library, a body hit mine and I automatically recoiled the way I had since my return, making myself as small as possible and getting out of the way as much as possible. Usually, they paid me no mind and went on their business. But this body didn't move on like the bodies always did.

"Long time no see, *piccola nuvola*," said a smooth deep, Italian voice and I felt it in places I didn't know existed anymore.

I looked up through my hair and there he was. Staring right at me like there was no place I could ever hide from those piercing pale brown eyes. A shiver ran through me, and a teasing smirk lit his gorgeous face.

Because whatever else he was, Dante Wolfe *was* gorgeous.

Already six feet or taller with wide shoulders, contoured muscles, and tattoos that were obvious even under his white school shirt, he strode through life with the arrogance of a man who was used to being obeyed. His near-black hair hung into his eyes but was shorter at the back and sides. Since school had gone back, he'd had a smattering of dark stubble over his square jaw that made him seem so much older, more dangerous, and more delectable than he already was. His eyes were almost golden, with a darker circle around the outside and framed by dark lashes, and it seemed they could see into a person's soul. Completing the package that, like the rest of the students at Lionswood, only loosely adhered to school uniform code, he had a barbell piercing in his left eyebrow and an industrial barbell at the top of his right ear.

But it wasn't just the visual of Dante Wolfe that was pleasing. He exuded an air of heightened sexuality that told you he'd have you screaming his name with very little effort. He dripped raw sexuality that I couldn't help but pay attention to, be drawn to. He had an easy confidence without it straying into cocky territory, because that man had earned it.

The Lord of the Immortals.

He intimidated. He bullied. He wasn't afraid to assert his dominance with well-placed words or fists. He was just the kind of guy I'd sought out these last few months, the kind of guy I'd recently realised got my motor purring. The only difference to those other, insignificant guys was that Dante Wolfe had a keen intelligence glinting in his eyes that got that motor absolutely roaring.

And it was an intelligence that was directed right at me.

"I see your absence didn't help your timid meekness, *principessa*," Dante said as he took a step towards me.

I was already close to the wall, and I cowered into it. For all the training I'd put myself through before my return, my witty retorts stayed firmly in my head. I was conditioned in these halls to be that meek and mild idiot. Well, not for much longer.

"I see you still haven't grasped the concept of personal space," I forced myself to say to him.

"*Guarda*, I know all about personal space," he purred as he took another step closer. "How else could I perfect invading yours?"

I felt myself frown. But it was only on the outside. No one had ever looked at me the way Dante was looking at me. Not before everything changed, and certainly not a single time since.

He reached up, wrapping a front strand of my hair around his finger to lift it away from my face. He looked at me. Really looked at me. The backs of his fingers brushed against my cheek – my scar – gently.

"That looks good on you," he said, and it flipped something inside me.

I wasn't as strong as I wanted to be, but it was a start. "You like your women disfigured?"

"I like them *forti*. Strong. You survived. You should be wearing it with pride."

"It's not a badge of honour."

He shook his head. "No. It's a beacon. A fucking neon sign."

"And what's it telling you?"

He leant down so his lips were close to my right ear. "To not fuck with you."

"Which you plan on ignoring?" I guessed.

My hair still wrapped around his finger, he pulled ever so slightly, making my head tilt to the left. Something pooled deep in me. Something dangerous. Something that had no right being there.

Dante leant closer to my exposed neck and that something didn't just pool, but it zinged. I felt the proximity of his nose as it blazed a trail up my neck without even touching me.

My chest tightened.

There were parts of me that remembered the fear of that day ten months earlier. Parts that threatened to relive it. There were more parts of me ready to fight. If I went down again, it wouldn't be without leaving a permanent mark on whoever dared hurt me again.

"I can't ignore it," Dante said, his voice low and husky. "*È una sfida*. It's a challenge. A call. You're marked, *piccola nuvola*, in more ways than one." He fisted my hair and pulled my head back to force me to look up at him. "Only time will tell if that…" His gaze dipped to my scar and back to my eyes, "crack is just the beginning."

"You won't break me," I told him, feeling stronger than I sounded.

A vicious pleasure shot through his eyes. "Maybe not, *principessa*, but I'll enjoy trying."

And with that, he was gone. My hair released without so much as the smallest pull or tug or pain.

Leaving me standing alone in the corridor, my heart thudding loudly in my chest. Only, the erratic staccato wasn't just adrenalin. Not just fight or flight. There was something else squirming in the dark recesses of my newly forged soul. Something infinitely more dangerous than gaining Dante Wolfe's attention; the desire to keep it.

Chapter Four

Dante knew I was back.

The man who hated me, for nothing more than my birth and the associations that birth automatically linked me to, knew I was back at Lionswood Academy and…

He hadn't done anything.

Nothing more than he'd done before I'd run into him. Though, I was starting to believe that hadn't been an accident. I was also starting to believe that he *had* been watching me from the first week back in the dining hall. He'd seen me. He'd recognised me. My paranoia had been justified.

And yet, he'd done nothing. Except now he caught my eye with a knowing glint in his like we shared a joke. I was pretty sure the joke was going to be on me sooner rather than later. And it had the power to be deadly.

As far as I could tell, even Riker didn't know I was back.

But why not?

Why hadn't Dante thrown me to the floor in front of the Elites, broken and bleeding, and made a big deal as to how dumb they were to not have noticed Raine-fucking-Edwards, their discarded princess, had returned?

I could only conjecture. I certainly wasn't going to give the Lord of the Immortals of Lionswood the satisfaction of actually asking him. The lengths he'd hold it over me if he thought I cared! All I could do was hunch over on myself further and hurriedly change direction whenever I saw him.

On Sunday, I was trying to sneak out of the dining hall after lunch when I saw Dante. His eyes were pinned to me from his seat at the Immortals table as he moved his lunch around with his fork. His lips moved effortlessly as he spoke, but I didn't know who to or what about. Annoyingly, it was pleasant.

Something horribly bright sparked in me for a second as he put his fork in his mouth, dragging his teeth over it in a way that made me wonder what it felt like to have him drag them across my tender skin. A delicious curl of something dark writhed deep in my stomach, and even further down. I was sure he couldn't tell, but there was a flash of deeper teasing and knowledge to his eyes, even from the other side of the room.

My heart fluttered in my chest in a way that felt foreign, forgotten, and terrifying. I pushed my way out of the room, not caring who or what I ran into with my hair in front of my eyes. But no one said anything other than the usual 'oi,' or 'watch it,' to indicate they thought nothing more of me than I was rude and an unmemorable blip on their weekend.

As I headed across the quad, I tried to force my heart to calm down. It beat ragged in my chest with the potential for things I didn't want to remember, let alone feel again. On the other side of the quad, I took refuge against the wall of the Vitelli Building as I slowed my steps and looked up to the sky to calm myself.

After a few deep breaths, my heartbeat was back under control, and I could tell myself once more that Dante Wolfe didn't affect me. I dropped my head to see where I was going, and I realised that I'd dropped my guard for too long. Panic gripped me again in a very different way.

West was ahead, walking towards me presumably on his way to lunch. He was surrounded by Talulla, Fletch, Zak and

Olivia. They all looked perfect and beautiful and carefree as they always did. The boys were in chinos and button-down short-sleeve shirts, and the girls wore cropped trousers and blouses with heels no one actually needed to even have on campus, let alone wear.

I almost thought I was going to get away without them noticing. I was the only other person in the vicinity, and they were probably going to look at me at some point. But it looked like they weren't going to be any the wiser of my identity.

But then the world was clearly against me.

As his eyes roved the path, West's eyes just happened to fall over me right as the breeze lifted my hair from my face. I froze. Then, two heartbeats later, I saw the recognition light his eyes, even from that distance. I saw the surprise. The calculation. Then the determination in the wry tilt to the side of his lips.

I readied myself for him to reveal me to the others with him.

Flight would do me no good here and, for all the work I'd put in, fight would no doubt be proven just as useless. My heart was trying to crawl out of my throat and break a hole through my chest at the same time. My hands shook and my knees were quite ready to buckle; if I was on the ground first, then West and his buddies couldn't put me there.

West's mouth moved, but none of them looked my way. His eyes didn't leave me as they approached. As though organically, West manoeuvred himself so he was the closest to me. As was habit, I swerved closer to the nearest wall and prayed my joints would keep me standing. But there was nowhere else to go. I couldn't get any further away from him short of turning and running. And that would have been worse when he caught up to me. Because he would follow, and no amount of daily running regimen would save me; he would catch me, and he would punish me.

As he got closer, I saw the look of victorious triumph twisting that handsome face into a mask of horror and ugliness. Such hatred. Such disgust. Such superiority. Such a warning of the pain that awaited me and the joy it would give him.

West shoved me back into the wall as he passed, like I was no different to any other outsider, and walked away laughing. I wished I could say I didn't feel small and helpless. I wished I'd been strong enough to at least push him back or something. I'd thought I was – that I would be – but, faced with him again… I'd failed myself.

"Say the word, and he's *morto*," Dante fair melted in my ear, appearing out of nowhere as West and the others disappeared around the corner.

I didn't know a lot of Italian – or really, any – but I could guess what 'morto' meant.

"I can save myself," I told him, still watching in case West came back.

"Can you?" he teased.

His breath on my neck sent goose bumps skittering over my skin, it sent my heart beating into overdrive. So similar to the way West made me feel but so different as well; it made me want to lick my lips and press my body back into the inviting warmth of his at my back. But I kept my eyes on the corner of the building and focussed.

"Let me save you, *principessa*," he begged. I could also guess what 'principessa' meant and I was going to take that as the insult it was no doubt meant.

"You're not knight in shining armour material, Dante," I said flippantly.

"*È così*. Aren't I?"

I turned to him and looked him up and down. "Let me

rephrase. You would never stoop to being anyone's knight."

His silence about my return made me feel an unbidden and unwanted bond with him that gave me a courage of sorts to speak my mind. He didn't make me nervous or uncertain or inferior or afraid the same way West or anyone else did. I knew it was inadvisable and undoubtedly setting myself up for his retribution, but it was like I was on autopilot around him.

He pressed a hand to the wall by my head as his eyebrow disappeared under the hair hanging over his forehead. "Is that what you think of me?"

"Why do anything for anyone if you get nothing in return?" I asked sarcastically, finding myself leaning into him.

He smirked and leant forward so his lips were by my ear. "Who said I'd get nothing in return?"

Dante pulled back with a wicked and sinful grin, one that twinkled in those golden eyes and made my stomach do funny things. Before I could think of anything to say, he winked at me and walked away.

I watched him go with something that burrowed deep in me.

I knew it was him.

It was Dante.

He was effortlessly sliding past every one of my warnings and defences. All those systems I'd spent the last ten months growing and building and strengthening. He was in before I could stop him, and I couldn't bring myself to push him back out the whole way. Like I was leaving a way in for him for next time. Like I wanted him in there. Which was ridiculous because I didn't want him there. I couldn't afford to have him there.

I'd returned to Lionswood for one purpose and nowhere in that purpose did Dante Wolfe figure. As it was, I'd been so wrapped up in Dante getting all up in my business and doing funny things to my stomach, it wasn't until the middle of the last lesson that I realised that nothing had changed for West discovering I was back.

I'd had my head so far up Dante's gorgeous, slappable, grabbable, tight arse that I hadn't even stopped to wonder what West's first act of retribution would be. I hadn't stopped to think that West should have spread the word far and wide and I should be dead by now, Dean's rules be damned.

But I wasn't. I was fine.

At least, as fine as I ever was.

Which was a pretty low bar, really.

Regardless, West had, just like Dante, kept my return to himself.

Like I'd entered some kind of twilight zone.

The panic of what that meant, once the implications hit me, was far higher than had West just announced my return and openly accosted me in front of the whole school. The panic was higher than when Dante had done it because West was far less stable, far less reliable. His motivations and ambitions were totally random depending on his current mood. Just because he hadn't announced my return that afternoon, didn't mean it wasn't right around the corner. It didn't mean he wasn't just thinking about the best – read: most horrible for me – way of punishing me for daring to think I could be anything more than what they'd tried to reduce me to the year before.

But I wasn't going to get my revenge by cowering in my room or avoiding my lessons. I started keeping my blade in my bag at all times. All the closer for if West tried anything and worry about someone turning it on me be damned. I had no doubts that I'd come out the worst if West did try something, but I'd inflict as much damage as I could before I went.

After a couple of days, it almost felt normal. The anxiety. It was more familiar to me than the conflicting things Dante elicited in me when he looked my way. It was far easier to sit in the anxiety, to let the familiar patterns and habits and therapies soothe me so I could function in front of them all.

My pyschs would have something to say about me calling my methods 'therapies', no doubt.

But then, they weren't the ones trying to find a way to kill their ex-boyfriend before he killed them.

*

The next day, like he had some kind of camera or sixth sense, my father texted me. Not an email. Not a phone call. A text.

Dad
Tell me you've made
progress.

Raine
If progress is not just
West but also Dante
Wolfe knowing I'm back,
then sure I've made
progress.

Dad
How is that keeping a
low profile?

Raine
It's not like I just waltzed
up to them and invited
them for coffee.

Dad
Well, what happened?

40

> **Raine**
>
> I don't know. Dante
> seemed to recognise me
> from about the first day
> back or something.
> West...was more
> unfortunate.

Dad

Are you safe?

> **Raine**
>
> I honestly don't know.

Dad

Your mother will want
you to come home.

> **Raine**
>
> And you?

Dad

...

What do you want to
do?

What did I want to do? I mean, I knew what I wanted. But fear was threatening to overwhelm me. Fear of failure as much as fear of again feeling the pain and humiliation and betrayal. I had to force the panic away. Remind myself that I hadn't worked this hard to just turn tail and crawl back into hiding again.

> **Raine**
>
> I want to ruin him.

Dad

Do you have a plan yet?

Raine

I'm working on it.

Dad

Have you got anything?

Raine

I said I was working on

it.

Dad

So, that's a no.

Raine

What do you expect?

You kept me in the dark

about this stuff until

they fucked me over and

then you gave me a

crash course in the

theory but left the

practice for me to work

out for myself!

Dad didn't reply straight away. There weren't even any little dots to signify he was rejecting a whole bunch of responses before hitting send. When he did, it was unexpected.

Dad

Do you need help?

Yeah, I was surprised. I was surprised my father had allowed me to mouth off to him with zero reprimand, not even a warning word. He'd just asked me if I needed help…

Raine

No. I'm fine.

Dad

I will help you if I can.

42

                                    Raine

                                  I know.
                             I can do this.

Dad

...
There is such a thing as
being too brave, darling.

                                    Raine

                         Don't do that now.

Dad
Do what?

                                    Raine

                       Don't treat me with kid
                        gloves again. I'm not
                       your princess anymore.

Dad
You will always be my
princess.

                                    Raine

                              No. I won't.
                       I will never be anyone's
                          princess again.

Dad

...
Understood, darling. My
apologies.
             But you know
             what I meant.
Because heaven forbid a man in our world actually used the
'L' word, even if he would go to pains to tell you how he felt
while using ANY other word. Even a father to his only

daughter.

Raine

I do. Thanks.

Dad

Do not let me down.

And there he was. The man who was finally preparing me to be his heir. The way he really showed his love and his pride and his support. Treating me the way he would have always treated a son.

Raine

I won't.

Like, thanks, Dad. No pressure or anything.

Chapter Five

Like the cliché in every book or movie, I started taking refuge in the library. I didn't know who Wulff Iversen was, but he clearly had a buttload of money for the massive building they erected in his name. It was a huge maze with floor to ceiling chestnut shelves on multiple levels, full of more dark corners and places to hide than the Salisbury Girls Dormitory.

Obviously, though, not enough places to hide.

West and Dante both found me. Every day for the next week.

Whether they'd been following me or it was just by chance, I couldn't be sure. I did doubt that they'd be in the library for any other reason but me, though. Perhaps a bit arrogant, but a whole lot more realistic.

That day, West had been the one to find me first. He sat at a table in plain view of me, surrounded by other students at other tables, like he actually planned on doing his homework. He had his economics book out and held it in front of him like he was reading. I also pretended I was doing my homework.

Music was harder when you were being graded for more than your fingering. And, oh how I wished that was the punchline to a joke.

The top of my head prickled. I snuck a look up and saw West was still watching me. He wasn't even being that surreptitious about it, but no one else in there seemed bothered either by the King's presence or that he was staring at the unnamed, loner kid who kept to herself. Why would they? If the King of the Elites was letting them study in peace, they weren't going to do anything to jeopardise that.

There was a scuffling noise as Fletch nearly fell out of an aisle. I couldn't tell if he'd been running or if he'd actually tripped on something. He righted himself and looked around until his eyes landed on West. He dropped to a crouch beside his King.

"What the fuck are you doing here?" Fletch hissed at West.

All around us, eyes lifted on autopilot to shush the offending noise-maker, then dropped back down again in a hurry. All except West, who was still staring at me like looks legitimately could kill. The way my heart was pounding, I started to worry they could. I knew without a doubt that West Flintlock wanted me dead or, rather, as close to as possible without letting me off too easy.

"West?" Fletch hissed again, nudging West with his foot. "West?"

West blinked and finally looked away from me. Fletch tried following his gaze. I tilted my head so my hair hung further in my face, but I could still see them. Fletch's eyes scanned the library, but his face told me he had no idea what had drawn West's attention.

"What?" West snapped.

"What were you staring at?"

"Nothing." West's voice warned Fletch not to press the issue, not that Fletch would question his King. "What did you want?"

Using West's distraction, I silently packed up my shit and sidled out in the opposite direction. Before I completely slid away, I snuck a look back and saw Fletch and West whispering harshly to each other. I wasn't going to hang around and see how long it took for West to dismiss whatever Fletch was there for in the face of harassing me from a distance.

I didn't care anymore why West wasn't drawing attention to my return. Maybe it was a new game. Maybe he wanted to keep me for himself. Maybe he felt guilty about last year.

Ha.

As if.

But whatever the reason, it would only end badly.

For me.

As I walked, I tucked my books back into my bag. Or, rather, I tried. Until I turned a corner and saw Dante leaning against a shelf like he knew that was the route I took for the lowest likelihood of running into anyone. My skin prickled at the idea he'd been watching me, following me, memorising my routines.

Not all the prickles, though, were bad. Which only served to make me almost as annoyed with myself as I was with him.

"Stalker, much?" I huffed and I saw the humour light his eyes.

"I prefer the term protector, *nuvola*."

I wished I could say that wasn't attractive.

I wished I could say that Dante being intimidating wasn't attractive.

I wished I could say that he could throw me against the nearest wall like a ragdoll and I wouldn't still be thinking about how attractive he was.

Fuck, but I'd conditioned myself these last ten months. I'd had to, to survive. At least long enough to see West suffer the way I did.

So, yeah, I had kinks now. Kinks I'd never thought about outside a drunken viewing of *Fifty Shades* with the people I'd thought were my friends. Kinks that I knew, without a shade of doubt, that Dante would not hesitate to gratify with enthusiastic pleasure.

And, watching him watch me, I feared he knew. Feared that he could read on my face what I felt when I looked at him. But that was stupid. Dante Wolfe was no more mind reader than he was an arrogant son of a bitch who assumed that anyone he turned his heated gaze on would fall to their knees in front of him and beg him for the privilege of sucking him off.

I was not going to be that girl.

I shrugged wildly as I busied myself with making sure my bag would close. "I could *prefer* to call myself the world's foremost expert on cell division and it wouldn't make it true."

I heard a noise that could have been mistaken for a laugh and looked up quickly. The smile still lingered at Dante's lips. Those utterly kissable lips. Kissable and, I was sure, useful for other, lower things. But that wasn't what was currently holding my attention as I looked at him. It was the lightness, the glimpse of almost carefree simplicity in his expression that made me pause. It was too familiar, too personal. It gave the implication of a closeness between us that was never going to happen.

That flicker of bright spark threatened to flare in me, and I stamped it down furiously.

In aid of not giving myself away, I narrowed my eyes at him. "Does the Lord of the Immortals not have better things to do than skulk around libraries?"

"I happen to skulk very well—"

"You don't say," I muttered, but he ignored me and kept talking.

"—but I also know the little king sees you, *principessa*. He sees you and he watches you, and he dreams of touching you."

I scoffed. "West? Dreams of touching me?"

Any further conversation on the matter was interrupted by West himself.

"I don't know, Fletch," we heard West growl from an aisle or so away.

Dante moved faster than light, suddenly pressing me into the wall beside me, like he was shielding me with his body. His very hard, large, commanding body. My heart pounded. Good and bad. Oh, I was worried West might see me – and with Dante-fucking-Wolfe of all people – but I was more excited about Dante's body hard up against mine.

Dante's face dropped slightly so it was right by mine, and we stared into each other's eyes like we shared a secret in both hiding from West. But it was more than that. Far more dangerous. It felt like it was forging a connection in something far stronger than stone between us and I was powerless to stop it.

As I stared into Dante's beautiful golden eyes, my heart stopped pounding in fear. The anxiety was leaving me. Oh, my heart still thudded. My every nerve felt alive and on the precipice of fight or flight. I was full of a restless energy that just begged to be put into action. Any action.

But I didn't care about West finding me anymore.

A shield, indeed.

I didn't have the mental space to worry too hard about West when Dante was standing there against me, and my hand had found its way to his chest, very definitely not trying to push him away. The need to worry about West in that moment diminished as I was flooded with the very real sense that Dante would protect me against him. Not that I needed him to, but no one had ever made me feel that way ever before.

"He dreams of touching you, the way I dream of touching

you," Dante whispered, his nose trailing across my cheek, only just not touching it at all.

My nipples pinched at the intimacy of the moment, at the hinted promise of more, at the idea that Dante dreamt of touching me.

"I would hope they're very different dreams," actually came out of my mouth in what could only be described as a breathy, seductive moan.

Dante's hand went to the wall at my hip, and he swayed into me as his lips dipped to my ear. "We are both the product of our world."

I stiffened. "Do *not* make excuses for him," I snarled, but his hand very briefly skimmed up my side.

"I do not. I make excuses for me."

My heart wasn't the only thing thudding and I had to swallow before I could answer because it wasn't fear that gripped me when he said that.

"Why?" I asked him and he pulled his head back only enough to look into my eyes again. "What exactly do you dream of doing to me, Dante?"

I don't think I could have sounded more like I was begging for it if I'd actually literally begged him for it. But, instead of looking at me with sympathy like I was hilariously pathetic, his eyes dripped heated desire as they looked me over. He wasn't afraid of maintaining eye contact, that was for sure. He was sure and confident. It was a surety and confidence I didn't think, for all the power he threw around, even West had in him.

"I think you know, Raine."

"Would it hurt to tell me?"

"I could tell you. Or I could just show you."

Something swirled around us. Between us. Something new. Something that made my heartbeat quicken and heat pool between my legs. For the first time in a long time, I felt something other than the loneliness of pain and retribution. And the Lord of the Immortals was the one to bring it out in me.

I was reaching up towards him.

He was leaning down to me.

Everything in me was telling me that his lips – and more – were the answer. They were the switch that would make it all go away. At least for a while. They were the key to even just a moment of respite. It wouldn't be any healthier or safer than what usually kept me running, but maybe it would feel better. At least in the moment, it could feel better.

I knew it like I knew my own name. This thing between Dante and me could provide distraction. But I couldn't afford distraction. I was on a mission and even the promise of untold pleasures wasn't enough to make me stray from the path.

Still our lips inched closer together.

I saw the cheeky arrogance in those eyes of liquid gold as he looked down on me through his hair. My fingers itched to run through that hair, for a moment behaving as though we could afford the luxury of crushes and romance and anything sweet.

There was nothing sweet about Dante Wolfe, even if we'd had the time. And I wouldn't have wanted sweetness from him either way. Were I going to indulge in the fantasy of giving myself to Dante, I would have wanted him to show me how good bad could really be.

I'd want passion.

I'd want burning desire.

I'd want him to fuck me six ways from Sunday, and in the chapel no less.

I'd want him to explore every inch of my body and still

leave me craving more.

If I'd wanted Dante.

Which I didn't.

So, I pressed my hand harder to his very firm chest and told him, "You come any closer and I'll make your face rival mine."

His grin was all smug and sexy conceit, but he didn't come any closer. "No face could rival yours, *piccola nuvola*. You were already beautiful, but your strength… I see your strength blazing in your eyes and that is what gets my cock hard."

That was very tempting. But I leant towards him, reaching up so our lips were dangerously close, and said, "I'm still not going to kiss you."

He leant in so his nose brushed mine. "Maybe not today."

His voice was low. Sensual. It caressed my skin. But I'd fallen for the tricks of a King. I wouldn't fall for the tricks of a Lord.

"Not ever," I promised him.

He took a step further into me, forcing me back into the cold stone. "Do not think I will make the little King's mistake, *principessa*," he growled. "I'm not stupid enough to let you go."

"I'm not yours to *let* go, Dante."

"You will be."

"Nothing will ever happen between us."

"The only time a *Plutonis Satellites* gives up pursuit is when he's dead and, even then, grown men know to keep one eye over their shoulder."

"Then maybe I'll just send you down to meet your god," I suggested.

Molten heat made his golden eyes shine.

West wouldn't have stood for such blatant disrespect.

Dante liked it. He enjoyed it. It turned him on.

"You wouldn't have spoken to him like this last year, *cara*," he said softly.

"I wouldn't have spoken to anyone like this last year," I reminded him, equally as softly.

"So, it's just me?" He looked unbelievably excited by that idea.

His excitement excited me.

He was definitely the only one I'd speak to like this. I wasn't putting myself in any situation where I had to speak to anyone at all if I could help it, let alone like this.

"Do you feel special?" I asked him, trying to deny everything I was feeling around – for – him.

His knee pressed between my legs. Not enough that he was trying to force my legs open, but enough to tease me. To test me. I couldn't be sure if I passed or failed. That might depend on which of us you asked.

"I am special," he told me. "Because you are mine."

My heart leaped into my throat, just the distraction he needed to stop me articulating a reply. That is, had my brain not short-circuited and been able to formulate one. There was something very off-putting but also comforting about his conviction, and there was a part of me – probably that fucking little bright spark – that couldn't bring myself to push it away.

He smiled like he, again, knew what I was thinking.

Then he gently pushed away from me.

"It sounds like the little king has gone."

He didn't so much say outright that I was safe now, but I felt it.

Standing in front of the Lord of the Immortals, a man who had only got where he was by adding who really knew how many names to the Orders of Service in Foxfield Hall, I felt safe.

After everything I'd done in the past ten months to try to regain that feeling once more, my mind rejected the idea that he could give it to me so effortlessly and seemingly so freely.

I grabbed my bag strap tighter over my shoulder and ran, trying to leave the feeling behind me. Trying, in vain, to tell myself that there was another explanation, that I was confusing lust for something else.

By the time I got to my room, I'd successfully reminded myself that Dante was no better than West. He was, if anything, worse. He was simply far better at playing the game than West could ever hope to be.

Chapter Six

The next morning, my hand shook as it reached for my bedroom door handle. Now I was about to step out the door, I was less sure I could do it.

I'd woken up and told myself I could do it.

I'd got out of bed and told myself I could do it.

I'd got dressed and told myself I could do it.

But the shaking of my hand told me I didn't believe myself.

I just couldn't put off a run any longer.

I was going mad, cooped up within these walls, never knowing if someone or something was coming for me. It had become clear to me that neither Dante or West were going to draw attention to my return. I'd given up caring why for either of them, but I knew it in the very fabric of my being that they'd keep it to themselves for as long as possible. To what end, I was still waiting.

But waiting was driving me crazy.

I needed something more than I was getting in relief. I needed fresh air as well as endorphins. So, I had to run. I'd set my alarm for five, thinking that would be plenty of time to get out, have a decent run and get back before even the earliest risers would be about. And, hopefully, it would be late enough to miss the night-owls.

I just stared at my hand shaking, millimetres away from the doorknob, and willed it to just fucking do its job. I was stronger than this. I had to be. I refused to give into my demons until those demons were six feet deep and couldn't hurt anyone else either. Before that, I would rise above it and get the fuck on with it.

Finally, my hand snatched at the knob and opened it. I slipped the key into my sport bra pocket and slunk out into the dark hallways.

Lionswood Academy was an eerie place at the best of times. It was old. Centuries old, full of any number of 'fixes' and additions and extensions and renovations but, at its core, it was a bunch of medieval buildings that were drafty as fuck and dark, even in the middle of the day at the height of summer. In the wee hours of – whatever the opposite of twilight was – as we were very firmly in Autumn, it was by pure muscle memory that I didn't fall on the stairs and put myself out of everyone's misery.

I'd had less chance to learn the roots and the paths among the trees, so I went slow and didn't push myself. The air was brightening with every step but, I was still surrounded by shadows.

As I paused to get my breath, I thought I heard something in the woods with me. Not quite the snapping of a branch or the rustle of leaves against shoes, but the definite sounds of movement made by something decidedly larger and more corporeal than wind.

I looked around, but knew it was a futile gesture. There were a million places to hide in here. In hindsight, coming in here had just been a very loud call for someone to follow me and make use of that 'How to Dispose a Body 101' class.

Wiping my arm over my top lip, I casually glanced around again.

I could feel someone out there. Someone was watching me.

I didn't know how long they'd been following me, and I didn't know what their intentions were. Strictly, the woods could be argued to be off school grounds. It had worked as a defence once. It had failed more times, but that one time was all that was needed that, if someone really wanted me dead – *looking at you, West* – then they could follow me out here and that would be it.

Besides, the punishment for killing a student on school grounds was highly dependent on the situation. The idea of a little expulsion didn't usually bother a lot of the kids here; it wasn't like their parents couldn't get them into whatever school they wanted anywhere in the world. But being expelled from Lionswood – or any of their affiliate schools – came with a buttload of ramifications and stigmas.

Only the worst of the worst got expelled from a place like Lionswood.

And not in a good way.

The kids who weren't tough enough to do what needed doing.

The kids who weren't smart enough. Usually to not get caught.

The kids who didn't lie or cheat or steal or kill.

The kids who ended up dead and broken and no one's problem anymore.

I'd known plenty of them in my time at Lionswood. They may have tried to keep me sheltered and naïve – and for the most part it had worked – but there were things that were impossible to miss. There were things that, in hindsight, it was impossible not to understand now that I had more pieces of the puzzle. The world was kill or be killed…unless you were breeding material. And I wasn't going to be breeding material by the time I was done.

By the time I got back to my room and changed, my anxiety hadn't really lifted all that much. It was better and I felt less claustrophobic, but the fear of detection was wearing me thin. Even when it remained obvious that I was in the clear. Or as in the clear as I could be with Dante and West shadowing me.

Later that day, it was West who found me first. In the library, far earlier than I'd given him credit for and I knew he was getting bolder about his notice.

I felt hands on me, using his whole body against my back to press me into the bookcase roughly. His hands gripped my wrists firmly, pushing them against the shelves so I couldn't move them. The smell of him was as familiar as it was terrifying. My heart thudded in my chest and my mind fought to remember everything it had been taught.

"Miss me, Raine?" that familiar crisp East Coast accent purred in my ear, but it was all threat.

I fought against him, but he was stronger, and I was panicking.

"Get off me, West," I snarled.

West's hand trailed to the bottom of my skirt, and I felt his fingers tickle my leg. I jerked in revulsion and thrashed against him harder. Oh, how I'd craved that touch from him a year ago, and now it made me want to throw up. He just laughed.

"I know you missed me," he whispered in my ear, like some mockery of tenderness.

"The hardness of your cock suggests you're the one who missed me," I snapped back, finally finding my spine. "What's the matter, West? Is it no fun when it's consensual?"

I'd meant to be teasing, but my blood ran cold when he breathed a chuckled, "Of course it's not," then bit my ear lobe like it was foreplay. He ran his nose over my neck. "I didn't think twice about you while you were gone. Now you're back?

I can't stop thinking about you. You were supposed to be broken, Raine. I didn't think you had it in you to pull yourself above it and come out stronger."

"You don't know me, West. I'm not the girl you tried to ruin."

"No," he admitted. "No. You're so much more, and I'm going to enjoy ruining you even more this time."

I shook my head. "No, West. It won't be me ruined this time."

I jabbed my elbow into his ribs and, while he was recoiling from the shock, I ran, wishing I'd had my bag and my knife on me. But then, what the fuck would I have actually done? I wasn't actually going to risk giving him a chance. I couldn't take him in a fair fight, and I doubted the likes of West Flintlock cared about a little thing like the dean's 'all dead bodies off campus' policy.

As I was running, of course I ran – literally – into Dante between buildings on my way to the girls' dorms. Straight from the fire and into Hell.

His hands went around my arms as he laughed, "Where are you running, *cara*?" and I felt that flutter of something foreign and forgotten in my chest.

It was annoying enough that I'd left one tormentor to be found by another. Again. It was more annoying that my reaction to both of them was viscerally different. West brought out my fight or flight. Dante brought out my fight or flirt.

I pushed Dante away from me and tried to ignore what it might mean that he let go of me and let me step away. "I'm not sure why the Lord of the Immortals gives a shit about where I might be going."

The corner of his lips tipped, and cunning shone in his eyes. "It's not where you're going but where you're coming that interests me, *nuvola*." He paused, very much for dramatic effect. "Or when."

I internally rolled my eyes, even if I had less control over my physical body around him. "Get out of my way, Dante."

He held up his hands. "*Anzi*. Am I in your way, *principessa*?"

I wasn't going to admit – out loud – that he wasn't in my way. I easily could have walked away from him. Yet, I didn't. Why wasn't I walking away from him?

Something bright and glimmery seemed to try to flicker at the very edges of my consciousness, and I blocked it out.

I took a breath and, instead of agreeing with him, posed my own question as though it was an answer. "You always seem to be harassing me. Why is that?"

He took a step towards me, and my heart lurched, but it was, annoyingly, not unpleasant and it mirrored much further down. "I told you, *cara*, I cannot resist you."

"And *I* told *you*, you can't break me."

Humour made those golden eyes fucking shine, like they were gilded. "The fun is in trying, *principessa*." God, the way he practically purred at me. My whole body felt it and I had a feeling he actually saw me shiver at the unspoken promise in his words. It was a promise of mutual pleasure, not of harm, and I very nearly gave into it.

But I could hold my own. Maybe only against Dante at that point, but conveniently he was my main problem just then. "If you're so keen on breaking me, why the secrecy?"

He blinked, like he was actually confused for a moment. "What secrecy?"

"You only ever do this when no one is around. Embarrassed about what gets you off, *Lord*? Worried your kinks will make you look weak? Be enough to lose you your very precarious seat?"

His seat wasn't precarious, he'd held it his whole career at Lionswood. Not once had he ever been in danger of losing it. And the way he looked at me in that moment, he knew we both knew that was fact.

He licked his lip before taking another step towards me. I didn't step back. "Some things…" He paused like he was trying to find the right words. "…are better when they're not splashed around the school bulletin board. *Intimo*. Cosy."

I bristled. "There is nothing cosy about this – us."

Another step towards me and I felt the material of his blazer as it brushed mine. "Do you really believe that, Raine?"

In the privacy of my own mind? No. I was woman enough to admit I didn't really believe it. There was something addictive about this attention that Dante was suddenly paying me. Cosy? It was less cosy and more on fucking fire. It blazed white-hot between us with the power to burn me. Badly.

To him, I said, "All I'm getting is a chill." And I delivered it like I actually meant it. I was so proud of myself.

"I know just how to warm you up… For a price."

A thrill ran through me that told me I would happily pay it. Fuck everything that had happened, I'd pay Dante's price and them some. But I wasn't going to let base sexual instinct ruin everything I'd worked for, all my plans, the work I'd had to do to still be standing today, the work I still did every second of every day.

"There is no price I would pay for that."

He smirked. "*Non, cara*. I would pay you for the privilege."

Holy Jesus. Was he serious? "You have nothing I want."

Humour danced in his eyes, and it was mesmerising. "I have everything you want, *principessa*. You just don't know it yet." He looked me over like he was daring me to disagree with him, like he wanted the opportunity to praise himself some more. So, I didn't give it to him. When I said nothing, his eyebrows jumped for a second and he said, "You never told me where you were coming from."

"You mean, who was I running from?" I asked him, sensing that was going to get a rise out of him.

He didn't disappoint me. His eyes went dark, and I felt his whole body still. Like a predator just waiting for his chance to strike. "Who were you running from?" he asked me, and I got the feeling we both knew the answer to that.

"West touched me," was the answer I gave him, and I saw the snarl ripple at his lips. I decided to push a little harder. "He had his hands up my skirt while he promised to ruin me." My voice dripped seduction, but Dante and I both knew what kind of ruin West had had in mind.

Dante growled something in Italian even as he stepped even further into my space. "And you ran." It wasn't a question.

"I dug my elbow into him first," I said. A flash of surprise lit his eyes, but I couldn't be sure what he was surprised about. "Just in case you were wondering about what happens to people who touch me against my will."

Oh, I was talking an awful lot of courage for someone who'd been touched against their will not a year ago, and it had landed them in the hospital and permanently scarred — both inside and out. But I could put on the courageous mask around Dante. Even if I couldn't pretend to myself, I could pretend to him. I could pretend I was the master of my own destiny and my own body.

Like he was proving a point, Dante's hand alighted very gently on my waist, slipping under my blazer.

As though I was proving a point, I let him.

It was an horrendously dangerous game I was playing here.

Letting Dante Wolfe touch me. Letting him touch in the same moment I was telling him West's touch was unwelcome. It told Dante a million and one things he shouldn't be told, yet I couldn't bring myself to tell him to back off. I couldn't bring myself to warn him that he'd get an elbow in his side if he didn't take his hand off me.

I felt his thumb brush over me. Up and down. Back and forth. Slow and soft and…testing. He was testing me. My limits. Testing what I'd let him get away with. Because we both knew that's what this was. His eyes were asking me 'how much can I touch you?' and mine were replying 'give it a shot and find out'.

My whole body hummed at the idea he might do just that, right there. I wondered how far I'd let him get. Part of me knew I'd give him all of it. Whatever he asked or wanted or took. And I'd take right back.

There was that hint of something. It drowned out the rest of the world as I stared into his eyes and refused to question it. Every breath was slightly lighter usual. My mind and my heart weren't consumed with hate and anger and revenge. They were consumed with him. With the way he felt. The way he smelled. The way he looked at me. The untold pleasures he could give. The distraction he could provide. A single moment, as short as it might be, where I wasn't hanging onto the ledge of the despair inside me and convincing myself to just hold on until my job was done.

"What will you do to me if I kiss you, Raine?" he asked, his voice a mere broken whisper between us. "Where will you put your elbow? Or your knee?" His eyes flashed and I saw the excitement there again; the way my defiance turned him on. Even just the idea of my defiance turned him on.

I leant my body into his. "What makes you think I'll put

them anywhere?"

Desire pooled in his eyes as his hand tightened ever so slightly on my waist, and heat swept up my body. "I thought you'll make my face rival yours," he teased.

"Oh, but I couldn't do that with an elbow or a knee, Dante," I purred. Everything in me fluttered in anticipation. What did he taste like? What did he feel like? Just how *big* a distraction could he be? Or, after the build-up and the tension and the rumours, would it be the single most disappointing kiss in my life?

"I might not care what you do it with, as long as you touched me, *cara*."

I believed him. I believed this wasn't just him exercising a power over me and enjoying my reaction. This was him being as powerless as me to whatever pull was happening here. He needed me to touch him as much as he wanted to touch me. His eyes promised I wouldn't regret it. The way my skin zinged and tingled where he did touch it, told me I wouldn't regret it.

But what was Dante going to do once he'd had his touch, his taste? Would he ruin me the way West wanted to ruin me? Would he walk away like none of this had ever happened? Or would he want another taste?

And, just then, I wasn't sure I could handle if any of those were the truth.

Like he somehow knew I was about to bolt, he stepped away. "The next time you go for an early morning run, *nuvola*," he said smoothly. "You might think of better protection."

I swallowed. "You followed me." I wasn't sure if it was a question.

"I protected you."

I bristled and took a step back from him. "I don't need you to protect me, Dante."

I didn't need it, but that appreciation swirled in me unbidden. I could look after myself – or, I'd tell myself I could – but there was something vaguely pleasant in knowing that someone else was looking out for me as well. And he wasn't demanding anything in return. Not yet anyway.

"You might not need it," he said, his voice dark. "But you still have it."

I had no words to say to that. I just grunted in annoyance and walked away. He didn't follow me. He didn't call after me. He didn't force me to accept what he wanted and damn what I wanted. He let me go. I tried not to read too much into him giving me what should have been a basic human right, but it was difficult not to when it so starkly reminded me that he was one of the first ones to do so.

Chapter Seven

I couldn't shake it. Couldn't shake either West or Dante, or how they made me feel.

West made me feel so inferior. Still. Even knowing he was a grade-A piece of shit who didn't even belong on the sole of my shoe, I got caught up in our old dynamic. Him with all the power and charisma and determination to wear me down. A few years ago, his determination had been in wooing me. Now, he only wanted to break me so bad no one could put the pieces back together.

Dante, on the other hand, never made me feel inferior. I couldn't see him without something in me fluttering or heating or *wondering*. I got off on our arguing, our bantering. I got off on the fact that he made me feel stronger. I didn't know how. I didn't know if it was just because I could insult him and call him out on his bullshit, or because he obviously enjoyed it. But I felt stronger around him. A strength that was growing even when I wasn't with him.

Everything that flooded me when I saw Dante was both intoxicating and addictive, as well as setting off all the warning bells in my head. I didn't have time for distractions, but I was drawn to him. To it. Drawn to the moment of escape from the pit my soul had become. I wanted Dante almost as much as I wanted West dead. I wanted to not want him more.

Ahead of me, Dante was beating some kid into the wall.

His hand fisted the kid's shirt and tie, holding him so his feet scrabbled for purchase on the ground. The kid had both hands around the wrist Dante held him up with, but Dante wasn't fazed. I didn't know what that kid had done to Dante Wolfe or the Immortals, but I knew intimidation when I saw it.

I also knew a chance to not be seen by Dante when I saw it. So, I took it.

Scooting down between the two buildings, I only rethought my escape plan when I realised it was the perfect place for an ambush. Not a strict walkway, it only suited single file at most. If anyone had seen me, I'd be a sitting duck.

There was a clatter behind me, and I told myself not to turn, not to give in to intimidation. I wouldn't let them scare me. Not anymore.

"In a hurry, *piccola nuvola*?"

I told myself I didn't have to turn. Dante Wolfe was a danger to a great many people, but I had no reason to think he was a danger to me. He'd never once shown any hostility or violence towards me. Which was more than could be said for some people.

No, I didn't feel danger around Dante.

It wasn't the anger and pain and vengeance that had permeated my soul this last year.

It was something else. Not anything I wanted to name, but that didn't stop me craving even just a second of respite, a second where I didn't feel the crushing weight of what had happened. Even if the person who gave it to me was Dante Wolfe.

So, I turned. "Not enough that I half-arse my work."

He grinned, knowing what I meant. "He was given his penalty."

"Surely not," I sassed. "He could have easily walked away

but, instead of doing your job, you're chasing tail."

"I don't chase tail, Raine," he said and, were I not trying to be annoying, I'd have acquiesced.

"Oh, but I thought you wanted to *touch* me, Dante," I pouted sarcastically.

Heat flared in his eyes. "And I will, *cara.*"

"Will you now?" I asked and he nodded. "Well, go on then. See just how far you get before my knee goes hunting for soft bits."

"Oh, it's not soft, *principessa.*" Dante's eyes were burning as he strode towards me casually. "You'll find the only thing *soft* about me will be when I put my head between your legs…unless you want to feel my bite." He gnashed his teeth playfully and, oh, I wanted it. I wanted the soft and I wanted the bite. I wanted whatever he wanted to give me. I wanted to feel something else. Something this draw between us was promising me.

But I wouldn't give in. I couldn't. I had to focus on my mission. I wasn't going to be able to exact my revenge on West with Dante's head between my legs, even if Dante had the power to show me the gates to Heaven while he was down there.

So, strength. I would use that strength he gave me, and I'd throw it back in his devastatingly gorgeous face.

"You are insufferable," I spat through gritted teeth, whirled on my heel, and continued along the path.

I fought the urge to turn – fought the prickles on the back of my neck. I knew he was watching me, but I didn't know if he would follow. I didn't want him to follow me.

Except…

Except for that tiny traitorous part of me that had put a label to how Dante made me feel. The part that didn't want to just feel pain and anger and revenge all the time. The part that wanted him to give us a moment of peace. The moment he so clearly wanted to give me, too. Though I doubted he had any idea exactly what it would have meant to me.

I hurried into the school building, no destination in mind, just letting my feet take me away from Dante.

Which was a bad plan, because they seemed hell bent on taking me right to West. *If it wasn't one, then it was the other.* They fair fumbled for purchase on the ground as I forced myself to a halt.

It was futile to hope West hadn't seen me, but I did it anyway.

Before I could do anything, I felt a hand on mine. As he turned me to him, I heard that smooth, deep voice say, "Thank me later, *cara mia*." Then the fucker pulled me to him, and fucking kissed me!

In front of everyone.

In front of West.

In front of…

Dante's hand – the one not holding mine – went to my neck as he deepened the kiss, and my mind suddenly went blank in the most delicious way.

Everything fizzed and tingled.

My heart jolted in my chest.

Need spread through me like wildfire.

How had I not noticed he smelled amazing? And he tasted… I knew what he tasted like now. Like something rich and dark and decadent.

It seemed there *was* one sweet thing about him after all.

The hands that were clasped rearranged so our fingers entwined. Without my authority, my other hand fisted his shirt and brought him closer. His tongue swept between my lips to battle mine. The hand on my neck brushed up over my scar, then seared down my body, slid over my hip, and splayed on my arse as he pinned my body to his.

Thankfully, I was wrenched out of my mindless, craven need for Dante by the roar of a familiar voice.

"FUCKING WOLFE!"

That tone sent terror shooting down my spine, but it was Dante's smile I felt against my lips that made my eyes fly open. Dante's eyes were focussed behind me, and he was very happy with whatever he'd seen.

Dante pulled away from me at the same time he used our clasped hands to pull me behind him. As I turned, my gaze darted back, and I saw West's hand close over the empty space where my arm had just been. Dante couldn't have timed it better.

West stepped right up to Dante – chest to chest – and snarled at him.

The difference was striking.

West all prep school popular pin-up boy, and Dante every one of your bad boy wet dreams. West all blue-eyed and blond-haired, his clean-shaven face still with a hint of the softness of youth. Dante all gold eyes and black hair, and already all rugged man with a five o'clock shadow and tattoos peeking out of his uniform. Both gorgeous in their own way, but of such very different worlds.

"I will kill you," West seethed.

I couldn't see Dante's face, but I heard the humour in his voice. "*Per favore*, do your best. Give me the excuse to kill you."

"She is mine."

"You gave up your right, *sfigato*. I lay my claim."

"You think she's yours?" West scoffed.

"Tell me who is protecting her now?"

"Protection?" West scoffed. "There are far better pussies worth protecting."

I felt the entirety of Dante's body stiffen in anger. "It is that lack of intelligence that will see you lose. She is mine. Touch her and I will end you."

West leered in Dante's face. "You can't protect her every minute of the day."

"There are a great many things I can do for her – to her – that you couldn't, *piccolo re*." The insinuation in his voice had me almost thinking he'd actually done any of those things to me. I didn't blame West for obviously believing Dante had already done every single one of them to me.

I was sure I didn't imagine the flicker of intense jealousy in West's eyes as he snarled, "You watch yourself, Wolfe. She's barely recognisable now? Just wait until you see what I bother to leave behind. When I'm done with her, even your obvious lack of standards won't want her."

"*Vaffanculo a chi t'è morto*," Dante spat back.

Having as firm a grasp on the Italian language as I did, West growled back at him.

"Run along, little king," Dante sneered. "Without your muscle, I might dent that pretty face."

West obviously agreed with him, not that he'd admit to it. So, all he could do was say, "You'll both get yours", and stalk away like he somehow had the upper hand.

Shaking, I started to hurry in the opposite direction. But Dante easily caught up with me and pulled me into a darkened corner away from prying eyes and gossiping ears. Not that it was going to help, because too many people had just witnessed Dante and West having a showdown over someone, even if they didn't know who that someone was. Yet.

"Just leave me alone," I begged, my voice sounding as shaky as I felt.

West had already had it out for me. I just existed and he seemed to take exception to it. I survived his attack, and he was pissed. I returned to Lionswood, and he wasn't having it. And, now Dante Wolfe had marked me, West wouldn't stop until I was a broken shell cursed to live on in agonising torment; death would be a release, not a punishment.

Dante boxed me against the wall at my back. Oddly, even after everything, there was still something comforting about it. But that in itself made me uncomfortable.

"I can't." His voice was little more than a rasp.

Why were my eyes heating? "It's easy, Dante. Just walk away."

"I've tried, *piccola nuvola*. When you were his, it was difficult but I did it. After you came back, there was no reason. Now I've tasted you, it would be impossible."

"I'm not yours. I'm not anyone's but my own."

His smirk was almost sad. "You are mine, *cara mia*. The sooner you accept it, the more…pleasurable it will be for both of us."

I drew myself up as tall as I could. "I belong to no one," I told him more firmly.

He dipped his head and his lips brushed over mine as he said quietly, "You belong with me."

With.

Not to.

Together.

Not owned.

Against my better judgement, my heart did flutter. The surety with which he said that made me second-guess my disagreement. It wasn't just surety. He made it sound…right.

Not right as in factually correct, but right as in it – he and I – was meant to be. Like maybe we did actually belong together.

But, even if that wasn't ridiculous, it didn't matter.

I wasn't intending to survive my revenge. I wasn't looking to put down roots or find reasons to stay. And my mind was fully on board with the plan.

Unfortunately, it seemed my body hadn't got the memo because I reached up to Dante and it was me kissing him now. My arms wrapped around the back of his neck, and his wrapped around my back so it didn't matter that my feet barely touched the floor anymore.

As my lips touched his, everything was light and airy and warm. My body hummed and sang. It was a tune I was sure only he could hear, only he could answer, only he could understand.

My legs went around his waist, and he pressed me into the wall at my back. My hands were in his hair and, Jesus, but it was soft. Certainly softer than his hands on my body, igniting every single nerve ending and making me crave more. My heart jolted in my chest again, like it was restarting. It would be ridiculous to think that Dante's kiss had the power to bring me back from this half-death I'd lived in for ten months but, while his lips were on mine, I was more than happy to play pretend.

Dante's hand seared up my side as his cock pressed against me, eliciting an ache so deep in me that I bucked my hips against him and tightened my legs around him. With his body the only thing keeping me against the wall, his other hand slid up my leg and under my skirt. I felt the heat of his skin through my tights. My arms wrapped around his shoulders as our chests were hard against each other, and I kissed him deeper.

It was a battle. Our kiss. A battle where I both needed to

have and wanted to cede supremacy. No kiss had ever felt like this. I'd kissed West before the incident, but he had always been in control. I'd kissed many people since in my elusive search for normalcy, but they'd meant nothing, they'd been nothing. Nothing more than a means to an end.

Dante wasn't just a means to an end. He was the end. His kiss was the end. It was everything. Everything I'd told myself I didn't have time for. But I'd tasted him now and I didn't know how I was supposed to just walk away and pretend it hadn't turned my whole world upside down.

Our hips rocked together until we were practically dry humping against the wall. Hands roamed unabashedly, his fingers sliding under my shirt and raking across my bare skin. I felt the rumble of a groan in his chest and heard a whimper escape against his lips.

Then, as swiftly as it began, Dante was gently dropping me to the ground and stepping back.

"What are you doing?" I asked him, noticing that we were both breathing heavily.

He shook his head, a smile playing at his lips. "Not going any further here."

Why did big brains have to butt into this? Big brains had no business making sense and letting rationality prevail over throwing caution to the wind.

"You're passing up what might be your only chance on…what? Chivalry?" I scoffed.

He smirked, clearly amused. "Selfishness. And it will not be my only chance."

I nodded. "Yes, Dante, it will. That was it. One shot to get what you wanted, and you blew it."

He stepped up to me again and everything tingled happily but warily at the ice in his eyes. "I am not your little king,

Raine. If you think that's all I want from you, you have spent too much time with little boys and not enough time with real men."

It was him walking away from me this time. He left me with this feeling of humility, as though I'd disappointed him somehow. As though he'd expected so much more from me, and I'd let him down.

The something in me that he called to wanted me to go after him, to explain myself, make him look at me again the way he had only moments before. But he'd been the one to bring big brains into this and I was going to stick to that.

Chapter Eight

Dante had kissed me in front of people and people had noticed. They'd particularly noticed West's reaction.

The King of the Elites wasn't known for his cool head but losing it over some unknown entity had got people talking. It had taken them a day or so to work out that the unknown entity was me. That my body went with that body. That was the longest I could go before people noticed that Raine Edwards had returned to Lionswood because, once they realised that I was the girl Dante and West had basically come to fisticuffs over, they started paying attention and it had taken half a day before that attention had equalled recognition.

But thankfully, the initial reactions were confusion.

Confusion and constant staring at the scar running down my cheek.

Here I was, darker and possibly even more meek and mild, like some frightened mouse, hiding behind glasses and lank hair. I decided not to put anyone to rights over that. Quite aside from the fact that when it came to West and the Elites I may as well have been a frightened little mouse, it didn't hurt my revenge fantasies to have everyone underestimating me.

So, the question became, why in the Hell had Dante Wolfe been kissing Raine Edwards in the hallway in front of West?

It was a question that kept most of them from talking to me. Oh, they talked *about* me. They whispered, none too quietly, about me in front of me. Conjecturing. Coming up with hypotheses. Fuelling rumours. But never directly *to* me. They didn't need my input. They didn't want to know that it was something as mundane as Dante was using me as a pawn to piss off the King. They wanted it to be far more exciting. They wanted a sordid love triangle now that West's princess had returned because he must still be utterly in love with me.

So, the larger school populace wasn't a problem. Yet.

What was a problem was that Dante and West weren't done with their pissing contest.

West's secret was out and, worse, he now knew that Dante had had the same 'secret'. Worse still because Dante didn't just have the same secret, Dante had a better secret; Dante was 'allowed' to kiss me, to touch me without getting an elbow to the ribs. The rest of the school might not have known how long the two of them had known I was back before they all found out, but the King couldn't possibly be seen as being one-upped by the Lord of the Immortals. Not when it came to his princess. Not when most of the school probably didn't know why I'd left in the first place. I could just imagine West playing the heartbroken King after my disappearance. My shunning due to me leaving him. And now I was back and seen kissing Dante?

I could barely move through the school without people's eyes on me. Regardless of the fact my hair still hung in my face, I still wore glasses in preference over contacts, I wore no makeup, my scar shone starkly against my skin, and I still avoided people as much as possible. People watched me, they went to pains to bump into me in the hallways, no matter how small I tried to make myself, how inconspicuous, how much I stuck to walls and shadows. It was ridiculous how petty and unimaginative they all were.

West cornered me as much as possible, but then he found

Dante at my back and debated the sense in walking away.

"How long until West kills him, do you think?" I heard someone asking their friends. I wasn't sure if they knew I was in earshot or not.

"If they come to actual blows over her, they won't stop until one of them's dead," one friend replied. "And with the Dean's no bodies on campus policy…" They shrugged.

The third one looked around and I just heard them whisper, "But you know who'll win. I bet Wolfe could one-punch West to meet his god."

I'd had months of practice to keep my smile under wraps. So, even the Elites knew Dante would pulverise West without breaking a sweat. It was the only thing that had really stopped West from just outright accosting me; he knew Dante would be there and knew, as soon as he touched me, that Dante wouldn't hesitate to touch him right back and ten times worse.

It didn't stop West from trying, and a part of me had to give him kudos for that. Were Dante not on my side – as weird as that felt to even think – I would have been terrified of what West would do to me. Whenever Dante saw West, gone was the flirt and in his place was a stone-cold killer. I was actually surprised a little thing like the Dean's no bodies on campus policy was enough to stop Dante from just eviscerating West.

My whole existence was eyes on me. None more so than West and Dante. It was like I knew where they both were in any given room based on the level of heat and hatred boring into my person. And I was never wrong. If I looked up expecting to see West, I did. If I expected Dante, there he was. No one else's eyes mattered. No one else's touch mattered. I'd take the shoulders of every other student in there over even just the eyes of those two.

But I went about my life as best I could. There was a

definite spanner in my plans now. West wasn't just aware of my return but the whole school knew. Gone was the element of surprise. I wouldn't have been surprised if there was some app somewhere with a Raine tracker so West knew exactly where I was at all times. Because he always seemed to be there. In the background. I knew he was just waiting for the time Dante wasn't around to make a move.

As I turned a corner, my step faltered as I saw West walking towards me along the corridor, then I was being gently wrapped in strong, warm arms and Dante was kissing me. A few half-hearted catcalls sounded around us – those who assumed, quite rightly, that Dante was just trying to piss of West and were supporting his decision even if they didn't understand his methods. When Dante finally pulled away, and we were both breathing harder than strictly necessary, I saw Riker standing behind him with a look of pure, unadulterated ire on his face.

"Your Bishop doesn't like the game you're playing, Dante," I mused quietly.

Dante obviously didn't feel the need to look at Riker to confirm my words. "He is a little protective, but he is not in charge."

I licked my lip as I thought. "And when he decides to kill me because I'm causing too much trouble?"

"He knows what you are to me."

My eyebrows rose of their own accord. "He does?" I asked, not wanting to ask what I was to him.

Dante inclined his head. "He doesn't like it."

"I didn't picture you two as the rom-com movie watching, do each other's nails, and talk about your crushes kind of guys."

Humour sparkled in Dante's eyes as he looked me over. I

didn't really bother wondering what we looked like to those – possibly even still West – around us. My arms around Dante's shoulders, his hands on my waist as we stared into each other's eyes, a hint of a smile playing at his lips.

He nudged my nose with his and his lips teased over mine as he said, "This is much more than just a crush, Raine."

My heart did a weird thing in my chest that I buried deep. "Not denying the movies and manicures bit, then?"

I felt his smile against my lips. "The *Immortali* do not keep secrets from each other. My Bishop has been told what he needs to know to do his job. My *friend* has been told the rest."

My heart lurched and, despite the warning bells in my head, I still asked, "And what is the rest, Dante?"

"You are mine, *cara*, even if you do not believe it yet."

"And what will you do if I never believe it?" I asked him.

He took a deep, steady breath. "I would spend the rest of my life trying to prove it to you."

My breath caught and I swallowed hard. "Why?"

His hand slid up my side, my chest, my neck, to cup my jaw. "Because you are worth it." As he kissed me again, I told myself that I wasn't falling for it. I reminded myself he was just telling me what he thought I needed to hear to keep letting him piss West off by kissing me in front of everyone.

I wasn't falling for it, but it didn't mean I wasn't going to get some kind of pleasure out of it. I was more than happy to go along with Dante's lies because it gave me what I wanted. Sure, it pissed off West, but it also felt amazing. I could tell myself that I wasn't abandoning my mission for the sake of pleasure, because it killed two birds with one stone.

As I looked him over, I braved asking, "What do you expect to happen after you've been seen kissing the King's princess, Dante?"

"I expect the school to know who you belong with," was his smooth-arse answer.

"You're not just crossing boundaries here, Dante. I'm tainted. I'm discarded. I'm nothing. I'm even less than an Elite to the Immortals."

"If you believe that, then you have a fundamental misunderstanding of the *Immortali, cara.* You are not nothing. You have never been nothing. You are Raine Edwards." He said it as though Raine Edwards was someone important. "They discarded you because they were threatened by you." I scoffed and he frowned. "Do you not see your power, *nuvola*?" he asked softly, his nose nudging mine.

"I have no power, Dante. West controlled me. Now you're trying to control me."

I felt his whole body tighten before he let go of me and stepped back. "I don't want to control you, Raine."

"No?" My eyebrow quirked. "What is this protection racket if not a method of control?"

"Why will you not let me help you?"

"Because you don't want to help me," I told him. "Not really. You want me beholden to you. You want me to give myself up to you as some damsel in distress."

His eyes flashed anger. "Is that what you really think?"

"It's what I know, Dante. I've learnt a lot in the last year about how our world works. I'm not that sweet little naïve idiot anymore. I know the games you're playing. But I won't be a pawn anymore."

"No?" he snarled. "And just how do you expect to achieve that if you refuse to have anyone?"

"I don't need anyone, Dante. Especially not arseholes playing knight in shining armour just to get in my pants."

He growled. "*Bene.* If you want us to play the game, we'll

play the game, *cara mia*. You let me know when we're done, *si*?"

He didn't walk away, he just looked down at me, almost as angry as his Bishop was behind him. He emanated fury. His whole body seemed to thrum with it.

"What's the matter, Dante?" I teased, my voice low and seductive. "Not used to not getting your way? You want to put me in my place? Show me how to behave?"

His face twisted and he looked absolutely disgusted with me. "I will never raise a finger to you, *principessa*," he promised, his voice shaking with rage. "Never in punishment. Never in anger." His hand skimmed my throat lightly. "Pleasure is another matter."

I felt my eyes widen and I knew he could read in them exactly what his words made me feel. I wanted him to give me that pleasure now. I didn't care who might be watching the scene play out. I didn't care if they could hear us, no matter how quiet Dante was speaking. Whatever game we were now playing, I felt underprepared. But I'd been the one to push him into it and a thrill ran through me at what was coming next.

"Dante," Riker barked, sounding both bored and like he might throw up in his mouth at the sight of us.

Dante turned his head towards Riker, but not enough for his eyes to leave my face. "*Cosa?*"

Riker rattled off something in Italian, his eyes on me as though unafraid of reminding me that I was more trouble than I was worth. West's words hit me; *there are better pussies…* And I knew Riker was convinced of the same. He didn't know why his Lord was suddenly all over me. He didn't care, because his Lord's word was law. But he was just waiting for the inconvenience that was me to be over with. He was probably debating the sense in just handing me over to West himself.

Dante nodded and replied to Riker, then turned back to face me fully. "Don't play too much without me," he said, then pushed away and he and Riker disappeared.

West was still further up the corridor, absolute wrath curling off him. His eyes were dark and his arms were crossed. He was pissed. I just didn't know if he was more angry with Dante or with me. I got the distinct sense that he was jealous. He didn't want me back, I knew that. Even if there was a part of him wondering if he did, he didn't want me back. He didn't care about me. He cared about the power play. West cared that the Lord of the Immortals so flagrantly had his hands and his lips on the King's discarded princess and didn't care who saw it.

It was going to bite me in the arse at some point.

Because West had been right; short of camping in my bedroom, there was no way that Dante could protect me at all hours of the day. I was swiftly running out of time before someone actually came for me. Whether they found a time Dante wasn't there or they got bold enough that they figured any pain they could inflict before they were stopped would suffice, I couldn't be sure when it would come.

Running was out. Endorphins were all that was left to me. And even that wasn't taking the edge off so much anymore. My legs were raw, and was constantly wearing tights in an effort to hide the evidence, to protect it as well as to elicit just a little more pain out of it.

As I walked through the library a few days later, I felt the hairs bristle on the back on my arms. Tingles shot down my spine. Someone was watching me. More than one someone. I could feel bodies in the stacks around me like some sixth sense.

My heart thundered in my chest. I hadn't seen Dante since

lunch, and I hated that I'd come to rely on him for safety. I hated that my first thought when I felt threatened was 'where was Dante?' I'd come back to Lionswood prepared to fight and claw my way to my revenge, and here I was relying on someone else? No more.

As I passed an aisle, I saw Riker lounging. He had his arms crossed, but in such a way that I could see the fresh cuts on his knuckles. The fresh cuts that I had no doubt went with the blooming red on the cheeks of Zak on the floor at his feet. Bile rose in my stomach, but Riker did little more than incline his head to me as he kneed Zak in the head.

I looked between Zak's semi-conscious state and Riker.

"Afraid of a little blood, princess?" Riker snarled before running his tongue over his knuckles.

I forced a smirk for him. "Blood doesn't bother me, Bishop. You wasting your time bothers me."

His lip rippled unpleasantly. "Some would remind you it is a privilege being under the protection of the Lord of the Immortals."

I shrugged. "Some would remind you it's a bane to my existence."

"Any other girl in this place would throw themselves at his feet in gratitude."

"I'm clearly not every other girl in this place, Riker."

He took a step towards me, and my instincts had me taking a step back. His eyes shone like he thought that was the first sensible thing I'd done since I'd come back. "Dante is taking a risk on you, princess," he growled. "The least you could do was be thankful. Or shall I leave the little king's minions to break you next time?"

I swallowed as my eyes darted inadvertently down to Zak behind Riker. I forced them back to Riker's face. "I've told

Dante and I'll tell you; I don't need your protection."

Riker closed the distance between us. "I would be very happy to test your theory, Raine," he whispered, all threat. "But Dante has made it very clear no one is to touch you. Yet you stand here, daring to question him. Daring to be ungrateful to *me*."

"Why don't you kill me, Riker?" I said, my tone all seduction. "You so badly want to."

I saw the hatred deep in his eyes. So deep in his eyes I was sure it burned directly from his heart. "My Lord decrees and I will obey," was his answer. "But the first chance I have, I will end you, Elite scum."

I smirked up at him, pouring every ounce of cocky defiance I had into my eyes, all the more to annoy him. "All because I haven't dropped to my knees in front of your lord and shown his cock my gratitude?"

"Simply the cherry on top of the list of reasons I want to kill you, princess," he sneered.

I huffed a humourless laugh. "Are you really pissy I don't fawn all over your Lord, Riker? Or are you just annoyed that you can't enact any of the ways you've pictured killing me in the last five minutes?"

"I can hate you for more than one reason," he said.

I nodded and stepped away from him. "I have no doubt, but I survived what they did to me, Riker. I'm sure your *friend* has told you everything he knows about that, which I'm also sure is far more than I want him to know. And I'm not even going to wonder how he knows it. But I survived and I returned. If you're not careful, I'll deal with you once I'm done with West."

Was that a flicker of something akin to respect in the Bishop's eyes? Surely not.

Riker simply snarled at me, then picked Zak up by the back of his shirt and dragged him away. I lost my appetite for the library for the day and headed to my room to lock the door.

Chapter Nine

It turned out that Zak had been little more than cannon fodder. Sent to test Dante's reach and power. I should have known that West was both smarter and more conniving than that.

I'd thought being alone in the showers had been a good plan. Until Olivia, Jaz and Talulla found me, and it turned into a very bad plan. But then, a few spectators was hardly going to make them rethink cornering me.

While I was rinsing my hair, hands pushed me roughly into the tile. My head hit the wall and pain burst in my temple.

I turned quickly and saw the girls standing there with jeers and sneers on what would otherwise be beautiful faces.

"You think you could come back, and no one would notice?" Olivia asked.

Last year, she'd been my friend. As loosely as you could possibly apply that word. It had been her and Jaz at my back. Now, it seemed it was her and Jaz in front of Talulla.

I wondered for a second what the power dynamic was now, then Jaz slapped me across the face. I tasted blood. The stinging pain was enough to pull me out of my surprise.

Maybe I wasn't strong enough to take down my attackers yet, maybe they still scared the shit out of me, but these preppy, entitled bitches were not going to make me afraid of my own shadow.

"I managed it for half the term without you noticing," I shot back. Time to hit them where it hurts. "And you only noticed because West is obsessed with me being back."

"West couldn't care less about you, whore," Jaz said.

I smirked, my eyes on Talulla. "Is that so? Then why did he keep my return to himself for over a month?" I taunted them. It was three weeks. Close enough.

Olivia clearly didn't have words for that, so she just screamed and threw her hand towards my face. I caught her wrist, glaring at her. Her eyes widened in surprise, and I could see the uncertainty in them now.

I took a step towards her. "You'll find I'm no meek little mouse anymore, Liv," I said, my voice soft. "Hit me again and I will hit you back, and I guarantee it'll leave a mark."

I saw in her eyes just how terrible that plan had been. If I thought their retribution would be great before, it would be extreme now. But I wasn't going to take their pathetic jabs lying down.

Then Olivia and Jaz both struck out at once. Jaz clipped my lip as I avoided Olivia. I felt the heat at my lip to match the heat at my temple and knew they'd done enough damage. I took a step towards them, murder in my heart. They looked primed to take on whatever I threw at them, but a gaggle of other girls trooped into the bathroom, and they decided that a brawl in the bathroom with the whole lacrosse team as witness was probably less than ideal.

Olivia and Jaz hurried out, not bothering to check if Talulla was following them. But she was, giving a whole new visual to the scared little mouse. As much as I hated her for her actions the year earlier, I had to wonder just how much she was simply yet another pawn in the great chess board that West used to play the world. Sympathy tried breaking into my chest for her, but I stamped it down, making sure there was no other part of me that got dragged down with it.

One day I'd have time to mourn everyone West hurt, but not until survival no longer mattered. When I had my revenge, I could let the weight of his crimes set me free, but I was so far from that right now that I had to bury it with everything else.

I got dressed and, despite the incident with Riker and Zak in the library, said library was my first port of call. Like it had become the only safe haven in the school. Which was ridiculous, but I was painfully familiar with the fact that anxiety was rarely rational.

I actually managed a good few hours of study without seeing West or Dante or feeling unnervingly vulnerable. The heat at my lip and temple fuelled my anger, focussing my mind and making me unusually productive. So, by the time I was packing up to go back to my room, I was actually feeling a little bit relaxed. Of course, it stood to reason that the feeling would be short-lived.

When I looked up, I saw Dante was leaning on the bookcase across from me. We were the only two in that section of the library, surrounded by empty tables and low lighting. Who knew how long he'd been there. His hair hung over his eyes, so they were shadowed, but I still felt the heat in them. He pushed off the shelves and walked over to me before I had a chance to stand up.

As he looked me over, a frown crossed his face. "Who did this to you?"

I shrugged and found myself telling him the truth. "Some girls cornered me in the bathroom. I'm not sure who's going to regret it more."

He grinned.

"What?" I huffed, feeling awkward and naked under his gaze.

"You're fucking beautiful."

I scoffed as I stood up. "Uh huh. Split lip. Bruised cheek. To say nothing of the dead eyes and the big scar."

"Your eyes are anything but dead, *nuvola*," he said as he brushed his thumb over the split in my lip. My tongue darted out and drew his thumb into my mouth. I sucked on it for a moment and saw his eyes widen in pleasant surprise. "They are heat," he continued, his voice a ragged breath. "They are desire. They shine with light and life, Raine."

"I didn't think the Lord of the Immortals had to resort to lies to get lucky," I sassed, and his eyes flashed.

Dante stepped into me, forcing me back against the table, as his fingers danced up the inside of my leg. "You think I'm here to get lucky?" he asked, amusement warm in his voice.

"You told me I know what you want to do to me, Dante. Or were you lying about that, too?"

"I won't lie to you, Raine. I would find it hard to believe you don't know what I want to do to you."

I inclined my head. "And I would find it hard to believe you weren't constantly hoping to get lucky."

He smirked. "You're the one who sucked my thumb, *cara*." His fingers found the heat at my centre, brushing against me with the softest touch. My back arched into him, and my legs parted slightly. "*You* made this sexual. You started it."

"I can't imagine you're planning to stop it," I breathed as his fingers trailed over my clit.

His lips dipped to my neck. "Not unless you tell me to."

My hand went to his arm and my head titled to give him better access. It was all the consent he needed to slip his hands into my pants and slide his fingers through my folds. My hand tightened on his arm as I leant my forehead to his shoulder. I felt his smile against my cheek.

As his fingers stroked me expertly, his other hand touched under my chin and tipped my face to his. Humour shone in his eyes. Not humour. Something more like joy. Victory, yes. But something that felt so much less selfish as well.

I reached up to him and, as our lips met, he plunged a finger into me. Both my hands gripped his shoulders hard, and I groaned against his lips.

He murmured something in Italian that I was pretty sure flew too close to sweet nothings. I kissed him harder as one knee bent to hug his hip. While his finger pumped me, his thumb found my clit and circled softly. I pulled him to me closer and felt his hips press against his hand as a second finger slid into me.

I took his lip in my teeth and his other hand tightened on my waist before sliding around my back. The back that arched into him as the pleasure mounted in me. As it did, our lips parted just enough to look into each other's eyes.

What I saw in Dante's made everything in me flutter in that foreign and forgotten way. It was both terrifying and addictive. He drew me in as that little bright spark tried guttering to life inside me. As we looked at each other, his eyes softened, like he could sense it in me, like he was encouraging that spark. And the spark wanted to answer him.

Not that I was going to let it. My hand went to the back of his head and my lips crashed down onto his again. His tongue swept into my mouth, both a battle and a surrender as his fingers worked me faster.

As Dante brought me closer to climax, my hands gripped his back, my breathing got heavier, and our bodies got closer. I leant my face to his as a moan escaped me, my hips rocking to his rhythm.

My orgasm crashed over me, and I breathed his name as

my body contracted around his. He stroked me gently as I came down, eliciting little aftershocks in me that made my whole body shiver. His lips found mine again and he kissed me softly until my breathing had returned to normal.

"I told you that wouldn't be my only chance, *cara*," he whispered against my lips.

I pushed him away and glared at him, straightening my skirt over my legs before he took his eyes from my face. "And quips like that will ensure *that* was your only chance."

He grinned at me, and it was so sexily lazy that, despite my recent climax, my clit throbbed for him, desperate for him to touch it again, for him to fill me up again. And not just with his fingers this time. His grin widened as though he could tell.

"It will not be," he assured me, more promise than threat. I couldn't bring myself to lie to him a second time.

"I suppose you didn't get what you wanted, did you?" I purred, running my hand over the very hard length in his trousers.

I felt him twitch under my hand, but he otherwise didn't move. "While I would happily bury myself inside you, *nuvola*..." His fingers caressed my chin. "Seeing you flushed because of me is enough." He paused. "For now."

"And what are you going to do if it's all I let you have?"

Those golden eyes shone with warm amusement. "Take it and be grateful."

Surprised by his answer, I chewed my lip. Finally, I asked, "Is this part of the game, then, Dante?"

The corner of his lips tipped. "If you want, *principessa*."

"And if I don't want to play the game?"

He stepped back between my legs, looking down at me with heat burning. "I think it's too late for that, don't you?" he said softly, his lips brushing my cheek.

Shamefully, I leaned into his kiss, nuzzling against each other as I told him, "Far too late."

*

The next time I went to take a shower, I found Vanda had followed me. At least, I assumed she'd followed me since her room – and therefore most convenient bathroom – was on a different floor.

She got undressed and into the shower two down from me in silence.

"You can tell Dante I'm surprised he didn't just follow me in himself," I told her, as though I was commenting on the weather or the temperature of the water.

"So am I," she quipped.

There was a smirk on her face and in her eyes, and a note in her voice I wanted no part of. It was far too familiar. Far too…affectionate. Like we chose to hang out. Like we were friends. And we were most certainly not friends.

We ignored each other as we got on with showering. Vanda seemed in no rush to finish, and I had to admit to drawing out my own shower to confirm my suspicions she was only there because Dante thought I needed protecting.

I stepped out of the shower and Olivia and Jaz were standing there, their faces set for intimidation. Honestly, they trooped all the way over to the girl's dorm bathroom instead of using theirs in the Manor, and all they were going to get was disappointment? Talk about shitty life choices.

"Nice day for it," I said, and they frowned.

"I thought you'd know better by now than to show your face in here," Olivia sneered.

"I think you'll find I know no such thing," I replied.

Jaz took a step towards me. "Then we'll have to impress it upon you."

93

"You can try," I told her.

"I think you'll find it'll be a fair fight," Vanda said, turning off her shower.

"I think you'll find I can protect myself," I said to Vanda, not taking my eyes off Liv and Jaz.

Olivia scoffed. "You think you can fight us?"

"You think I spent the last ten months just licking my wounds?"

Jaz's smirk made her hideously unattractive as her eyes darted to the scar on my cheek. "I don't doubt it took the whole ten months."

My hand shot out and jabbed into Jaz's nose. She recoiled, her hand going to her face as she glared daggers at me.

"Bitch!" Liv cried then lunged at me.

I dodged easily out of the way, spinning behind her and kicking her in the back of the knee. She went down on the hard tiles, and I grabbed a handful of her hair to pull her head back to look up at me.

"Touch me again," I dared her.

"You will pay, Raine," she snarled.

I grinned down at her, but it was anything but humoured. "No, Liv. Or are you forgetting how well I know you?" Fear lit her eyes as she understood the implication of my words; last year, she'd been my 'friend'. I knew things about her she didn't want other people to know. "Touch me again and *you'll* pay."

I threw her to the floor. She and Jaz helped each other out of the bathroom, stealing angry glances back at me.

"Shit," I muttered. "I'm going to pay for that."

"Girl," Vanda whistled. "You are amazing!"

I frowned at her as I went to wash Jaz's blood off my knuckles.

"No wonder Dante claimed you," she continued.

"I give zero shits what Dante Wolfe thinks I am to him," I shot back at her.

I'd expected her to respond like Riker; be all affronted that I dared to not fawn all over the illustrious Lord of the Immortals. She didn't. She smirked knowingly as she crossed her arms over her still naked chest.

"Oh, yeah. I get it now."

I turned to her. "There is nothing to get, Vanda. Dante will move on when my stubbornness gets less interesting. I'm perfectly happy using him for as long as I serve as amusement to him. Then we can both go our separate ways."

I couldn't tell if she believed me or not. Luckily, I didn't need her to.

"You don't think much of our lord's intentions, then?"

"He's your lord, not mine."

She was looking at me with new eyes. Like she'd never seen me before. On her face, I could almost believe I was as bright and shining and brilliant as her expression seemed to imply she thought I was.

"Did we just become best friends?" she asked, with a note of companionable teasing.

"No."

She grinned widely. "We totally did."

"We're not even friends, Vanda," I reminded her as I headed for the door.

"Not yet!" she called as I walked out.

Chapter Ten

It felt like, somehow, West knew I'd given into Dante. As though he somehow knew I'd let Dante touch me in a way West never had. Not that West had ever shown any interest in touching me like that when I'd wanted him to. Although, as I was starting to realise, my wanting him to was probably what made him uninterested.

But whether he knew what I'd let Dante do or not, West seemed even more determined to intimidate me, as though intimidating me alone was going to break me. Unfortunately, it seemed like it very well could.

I had spent the previous year strengthening myself. I'd prepared myself for coming back to Lionswood for the sole purpose of ruining West the way he'd ruined me, of utterly destroying him. And yet, every time I saw him, I was back to the helpless girl I was a year earlier. The one who didn't know what to do or say in front of him. He held a power over me that I couldn't shake, no matter how much I wanted to.

West followed me everywhere, knowing that he didn't have to touch me to intimidate and scare me. His presence and the mere threat of violence was enough. He hovered. It made trying to plan my revenge impossible. Every time I tried to formulate a plan, fear gripped me and I didn't believe success was even possible.

He watched me every time we were both in the dining hall,

his eyes drilling a hole right through me as he somehow managed to make eating threatening. I knew the threat wasn't just in telling me that he could destroy me if he wanted, but in encouraging me to keep not eating properly so I did his job for him.

Dante watched West watching me, a scowl on his face like he was daring West to make a move, daring West to hurt me so he could hurt West more.

And the rest of the school watched us all, too scared of West or Dante's retribution to do or say anything more than whispers behind their hands, behind our backs… Well, behind their backs. No one much cared about what they said in front of me.

Even the other kids at the loser table made sure to sit as far away from me as possible. They preferred sitting practically in each other's laps rather than risk being affiliated with me. But I heard them whispering among themselves, the self-enforced closeness making them far more chatty than usual.

"I heard she cheated, got pregnant, and had to leave to have the baby. Broke his heart," one of them said and my knuckles tightened on my fork. I cheated? That was low.

"Look at the way he still watches her. He *must* still love her." Oh, I had to roll my eyes at that. Loved me? He'd never loved me. West wanted to do a lot of things to me, but none of them were good.

"Isn't she with Dante now?" the third asked.

I actually choked on my drink, and they all turned to look at me. A couple had the decency to look somewhat ashamed that I'd overheard them talking about me. Most of them just looked like they were hoping I would confirm or deny. Amidst the coughing fit, I got up and stormed out, feeling the eyes of every student in the dining hall on me.

I felt a hand on my arm and struck out as I turned. Dante caught my wrist before my fist crashed into his face and smirked at me. My eyes were watering and my chest constricted with the force of my trying not to cough again.

"What do you want now?" I wheezed.

"I want to know what those *idioti* said to make you try breathing water."

I glared at him. "Nothing the rest of the school isn't thinking thanks to you and West and your…" I petered off as my eyes slid behind Dante to find West lounging against the wall, his arms crossed and his eyebrow raised like he was waiting to see what was going to happen next.

"Hoping to get you to himself?" Dante said and my eyes flickered back to him. His eyes roved over my face like he was looking for something.

"I think we both know he is."

"And yet, he's not coming any closer."

I kept one eye on West, and one on Dante. "Astounding powers of observation there. Your family must be training you up as a regular Sherlock."

Dante chuckled and I ignored what it did to my insides. "It seems the little king is not as stupid as I thought."

"Why? Because he knows you'll put your fist through him if he doesn't keep his distance? Self-preservation isn't intelligence."

"*Forse*. But not letting his base instincts get in the way of his self-preservation is smarter than I gave him credit for."

I scoffed. "And I suppose you know all about base instincts, don't you, Dante?"

"*Si*. Because mine are driving me to protect you, *principessa*."

Dante took a step towards me, and my eyes slid to West.

West stood up straighter, his hands dropping to his sides. I didn't know what he thought he was going to do about Dante being closer to me, but I was almost amused that he thought he was going to do anything about it.

"Well, mine are considering where I can put my elbow or my knee," I told him pointedly.

Dante's smile was wide. "Go on," he purred. "Touch me, *per favore*. Show him how little you think of him."

It was an enticing prospect, I had to admit. Use Dante for pleasure *and* for getting my own one up on West until I could find a more permanent way to put him down. It wasn't like the concept hadn't occurred to me before. It wasn't like I hadn't realised that was why Dante kept kissing me in front of West. I'd just not really thought about the implications of me actively letting him do so for that purpose. Of me getting that out of Dante. If I then initiated it in front of West.

But the school already thought Dante and I were dating. Did I want them to keep thinking that? Did I want to use it to my advantage? Or was it more important to make sure Dante didn't get any ideas about what this was?

Movement behind Dante drew my eye and I saw West had moved closer. Just what did he think he was going to do? He'd already walked away from Dante threatening to hit him more than once. What did he think Dante would do to him if he strolled on over? Invite him for a cordial threesome?

"It is your call, *cara*," Dante said.

My call?

If it was my call, I wouldn't be afraid of West anymore. If it was my call, I wouldn't be attracted to Dante. If it was my call, I wouldn't survive each hour simply by imagining the day I sank my knife into West's gut. If it was my call…

Maybe it could be my call…

Talk about driven by base instinct.

I pushed past Dante, my feet taking me very purposefully for once straight over to West. He planted his feet under him, crossed his arms again – expectantly – and the corner of his lip twitched as though he expected this to be good.

"Getting bored of the second-class sex, Raine?" West asked me, full of that cocky, arrogant charm. At least he wasn't hiding anymore. Long gone was the mask of kindness and sweetness with just a hint of shy awkwardness, the one he'd used to win me over in the first place.

Instead, his mask was haughty and superior, menacing and teasing. His power didn't lie in sweettalking me anymore, it lay in threatening me. It lay in me knowing what he wouldn't hesitate to do to me the first chance he got. My heart pounded and I was thrown back into that day almost a year ago. I felt the hands on me. Heard his laughter as he encouraged Zak to–

Fear.

Pain.

Danger.

...Run.

But I held my ground in front of him.

Anger.

Pain.

...Fight.

"If Dante's second-class, West, what does that make you? Third-class seems generous."

Revenge.

West snarled, but I saw the flash in his eyes. Oh, that was not good. That was the sort of flash Dante got when I insulted him, when I challenged him, when I defied him. It was the kind of flash that told me just how turned on Dante was. And it was smouldering in West's eyes now.

No.

Fuck. No.

I took a step back and West's lips curled. "Miss me as much as I miss you?"

My heart lurched and I hid it. "Yes. If you currently give less than zero shits about me," I said, my voice saccharine sweet.

Another flash in West's eyes before they darted up to Dante behind me. He licked his lip slowly. "How does your new *boyfriend* feel about you flirting with another man, Raine?"

"Man?" I scoffed. "All I see in front of me is a little boy playing prince."

Fire burned in him. "It looks like your face isn't the only thing that healed, sweetheart. I wonder what else you've been working on while you were gone?" His hand reached for between my legs, and I smacked it away, the bile rising in my throat. West looked behind me again and his smirk widened. "Oh, the Lord is taking his claim quite seriously, isn't he, sweetheart?" He chuckled. "How much damage do you think I can do to you before he reaches me? Just seeing you bleed could be entirely worth his punishment."

I took a deep breath. "Then, try it, West," I told him, my voice calm and steady. "Or do you want me to give *you* a reason to get a nose job, too?"

Humour lit his whole face. "Are you proud of yourself, sweetheart?" He dropped his lips in a pout. "Proud you could make Liv and Jaz bleed? Proud you managed to stop the big, bad girls from hurting you?"

"Do you want to see if I can stop you, too? You want to risk it? Please, go ahead."

There was a wariness in him as his eyes fluttered to Dante again. He didn't know what was between me and Dante. He didn't know how long it had been going on. He didn't know what we did in the dark. For all West knew, Dad had taken me to the *Plutonis Satellites* for training and that was how Dante and I got together. I could have spent the last year training against some of the biggest, strongest arseholes the Plutonis could throw me at.

I saw the debate in his head. Saw him trying to decide how far to push me with Dante standing right behind me. Could I inflict significant damage on West even before he laid a finger on me? Was the library a fluke? Was that elbow in his side just a taste of my new skills?

He didn't need to know that just the idea of hitting him made my hands shake. If I could intimidate him by just existing, then I was one step closer to my revenge.

I forced a smile for West. "You always did give into fear, West," I reminded him. Because I'd realised that in the last year; for all his playing at King and leader, West was little more than a frightened little boy who didn't want to drown under his parents' or our world's expectations. It didn't excuse the methods he employed to stay above it all. It just gave me ammunition to hurt him.

West took a step towards me, and I felt Dante appear at my back.

"Touch her and die," Dante growled.

I couldn't help rolling my eyes and West noticed the action. He spared a smile for Dante. "It seems the lady doesn't want *your* protection, Wolfe."

"I think that's for the lady to decide," Dante snarled.

West looked at me expectantly. "Well, Raine? Do you want Wolfe's protection? Or can you protect yourself?" The unspoken 'against me' was obvious in the way he looked me over hungrily.

Shit. Well, here was the definition of rock and hard place, frying pan and fire. I was under no delusions that Dante would keep up whatever this was regardless of what I told West now, but what would my answer to do West? What would my answer make him think he could get away with?

I could feel Dante's barely constrained rage behind me, and I wasn't sure how I felt about that. He wanted to pound West into the ground for threatening me. No one had ever wanted to do that before I returned to Lionswood. I didn't want to be the girl who swooned over a guy who wanted to protect her, but it was like this ridiculous primal urge to not only accept it but fall over for it.

The whole thing made a mockery of the person I had tried to become in the last year. The person I wanted to be. The person I deserved to be. I was working to be.

And, with Dante at my back giving me feelings I didn't want or have time for, and West at my front just waiting for me to dismiss my guard dog, I was pissed off. This was not how this was supposed to go. This was not how this year was supposed to go. No one was supposed to know I was even here. It had been less than two months and my cover had been blown by the one– two people I'd been desperate to hide it from, and then their bloody pissing contest had blown it to the whole fucking school.

I was still scared of West with no way in sight of actually ruining him, let alone killing him. I spent my life with eyes on me. Always watching, always judging, always wondering. What the fuck had I done to Fate to make her such a dick to me? How had I pissed her off so badly that I'd had to endure the year before and now I was even more powerless than I'd been then?

My hand flew out and smacked West across the face before

I knew what I was doing. His face whipped sideways, but he just licked the blood off his lip as he slowly turned back to me.

"Oh, I'd almost think I made a mistake throwing you away, Raine. But if I hadn't, you'd have never found this fire." He licked his lip again, as though he was savouring it. "I like it."

Dante growled and I nudged him back. His hand found mine and I don't know why they entwined in some silent message.

"So, you've made your choice," West said, noting our hands. "Interesting. I thought you were better than a dirtbag Plutonis."

"And I thought you were better than a piece of shit, West, yet here we are. I'd take a dirtbag over shit any day."

West locked eyes with Dante. "Are you sure *she* hasn't claimed *you*, Wolfe?" he asked, faux innocently. "I almost regret not tasting her if her pussy's so magical she can have you wrapped around her finger so damn easily." West stepped back, as though he knew Dante was going to step towards him, and laughed. "You're fucking weak, Wolfe. Throwing away sense for *her*?"

"You want war, *piccolo re*, you can have war," Dante told him.

West nodded as he started backing away. "No. No, I know. I touch her and I die. Sure. But you're forgetting one thing, Wolfe."

"*Che cos'è quello*?" Dante asked him and no one needed a translator for that.

West smile grew. "She will always be mine. And you touched what is mine, Wolfe. I think it will be you who finds themselves dead."

"Try it," Dante warned.

West just laughed and walked away. I forced myself to

breathe. I forced myself to relax the hands that had balled so tightly my nails dug into my palms. How could I have stood up to him and he still won?

"Raine–"

"Shut up, Dante," I muttered, and turned and walked the opposite way to the direction as West had gone.

"*Cara*–"

"What part of 'shut up' did you not understand?" I snapped, not bothering to tell him to stop following me because he was going to do whatever the hell he wanted.

"English is not my first language," was his excuse.

As we turned into a deserted quad, I rounded on him. I pushed against Dante, more for show than anything else. "I can protect myself!" I snapped.

"With what?" he asked, all teasing as he looked me over.

Yeah, I knew the package was probably not very impressive. I wasn't all that tall. I'd let myself get too thin. My muscles were defined from the exercise I forced on myself, but of no real threat to anyone. And I still started every time I saw West snarling at me.

"I have a knife," was my only defence.

"Do you know how to use it?" Dante asked me.

"Do I need to? You hold and stab. How hard can it be?"

Dante actually rolled his eyes at me. "If you're going to insist on being stubborn and pigheaded, I will teach you to use it properly."

"I'll be fine, thanks," I huffed.

Dante looked like he was swiftly losing his patience with me. "If you fight my protection, the least you can do is make sure you have your own. I will teach you."

I shook my head vehemently. "Oh, no. I know exactly what happens here."

He frowned. "What happens where?"

I stepped away from him. "No. Nope. Training montage? No, thanks. I've seen the movies. You offer to train me, hands all over me, one thing leads to another? No. Not happening, Dante."

I could not afford to be distracted from my revenge, even if it was a momentary lapse with lips that made my stomach bottom out just thinking about them. Those very lips twisted in a crooked smirk and made my stomach do just that. God, I wanted to taste them again. No matter how annoying he was, I wanted to taste them again.

"What happens in the movies, Raine?" he asked, his voice pure seduction.

I swallowed hard. "Not happening, Dante," I said again, ever so less convincing this time.

He stepped towards me. "Show me what happens in a training montage, *cara*," he begged – actually begged – and I had to take a deep breath.

"You really want to teach me how to use my knife, Dante?" I asked him.

His eyes went molten gold. "I'm intrigued about what happens in a training montage, *principessa*."

I felt my lips quirk and bit them to stop myself giving him a smile. "All right, then. You think you can hit me, *Lord*?"

"You think you can hit me?" was his humoured response, no qualms at all about showing me his smile.

I rejected the warmth in my chest at the sight of that smile. I rejected its attempt to burrow under my armour and form some kind of connection between us. But it sure tried its damnedest. I dropped my bag and bounced my eyebrows at Dante.

He lunged at me and I deflected, spinning to kick at his

knee. I grabbed a handful of his hair as his knee hit the ground and made him look up at me. Yeah, I had some favourite moves. The ones I'd practiced over and over again.

Dante grinned up at me. "If you'd wanted me on my knees, *cara*, you just had to ask."

His hand reached towards my skirt and I took it before he could touch me, even though I was wearing tights. He grinned up at me and there was a fluttering in my chest. How did I think this was going to go? Did I really think I could take whatever pleasure I wanted from him without him seeing my legs? And why did it matter if he did? What did I care? Of all the guys I'd been with in the last few months, plenty of them had seen, had felt them, and it hadn't mattered. They had been a means to an end.

I looked down at Dante, who had no idea why I'd stopped him touching me just now, and felt that end about him again. My heart pounded. It was fear. Not fear he'd hurt me or fear he'd let West hurt me. It was fear he'd see. He'd see the way I coped, and then he wouldn't look at me the way he was now. It shouldn't have mattered. I didn't have time for this feeling. I didn't need this feeling. This feeling had no place in my revenge scheme.

All I could do was shake my head, pick up my bag and run.

"Raine!" Dante called, and I knew he was following.

He caught me as I was shoving my way up the dorm stairs.

"Raine! Raine. *Fanculo*. Wait. Please, wait."

He pulled me to him and looked me over, concern marring his features. I pushed away everything that did to me.

"You don't have to talk about it," he said, his voice strangled. "But don't shut me out."

I glared at him and swallowed against the lump in my throat. "Shut you out?" I scoffed. "Dante, I don't want you in.

I don't need you *in*. This game we're playing? You're playing it by yourself."

The muscle in his jaw twitched. "You can tell yourself that you're not playing, *cara*. But we are both in this. Together."

"We are not together, Dante. No matter what the rest of the school thinks."

His grin was all predatory and it sent tingles shooting between my legs. "Would it hurt for them to believe it?"

"Yes," I told him. "It hurts me. I'm not being thrown away by the King of Lionswood just to be owned by the Lord. I'm my own person, Dante."

"Your own person who enjoys when I kiss you. When I touch you."

"The two things aren't mutually exclusive," I informed him snidely.

"So, you're just using me for your own benefits?"

"Like you're not doing the same."

He nodded. "*Bene*. Whatever you want, *mi principessa*."

"I'm not your anything, Dante."

"We shall see. I will be here if you need me."

I just snarled at him and stormed up to my room. True to his word, he could be seen loitering outside the dorm for the rest of the afternoon. Riker joined him after lessons finished for the day and they conducted whatever twisted business they did. I'd say one thing for Dante's obsession with 'protecting' me, at least it made Riker's life a living hell, too.

Chapter Eleven

Confronting West had quite possibly been one of the stupidest things I could have done. Not only because it made the target on my back bigger, but because there was that desire in West's eyes whenever he looked at me now.

I'd managed to get the one thing I'd wanted… This time the year earlier. Had West looked at me like that twelve months ago, I would have been the happiest – and stupidest – girl in the world. That West Flintlock wanted me as much as I wanted him. Now I knew without a doubt that the majority of the reason he wanted me now was because I didn't want him. I was a challenge I hadn't been a year ago. Not just a challenge, but a power play. His crown was in no danger because the school thought Dante and I were an item, but it would be a personal pleasure for West to have me under him.

West was hovering closer now. Still just enjoying the effect he had on me without actually having to touch me or invade my privacy. I hated it, but I was just pleased that it wasn't worse.

Then, as I lay in bed one night, I was distracted from thinking about West's hovering by someone who had no qualms invading my privacy. The privacy of my phone, sure. But it was enough.

Unknown
I found some training

montages...

Well, there went the need for my 'who dis' reply.

Raine

How did you get my
number?

Dante

The better question is
how long I've had it.

Raine

That's not a better
question.

Dante

Why didn't I get it from
you?

Raine

What do you want?

Dante

I'm just wondering what
kind of montage you're
avoiding.

Raine

Fine. I'll bite.
What are your options?

Dante

Rocky or Vampire
Academy

I choked on my water.

Raine

Movie or series?

Dante

Either.

Both.

You tell me.

Raine

What on Earth have you
been watching?

Dante

Whatever Vanda and
Riker and I
brainstormed.
We made a list.

Raine

You talked to people
about this?!

Dante

I leant on my friends, si.
And they are helping
me.

Raine

Why?

Dante

Because there is nothing
weak about leaning on
your friends.

Raine

No.

Why are you putting so
much effort into this?

Dante

I'm interested.

Raine

In what?

Dante
You. Your mind. Why
you're avoiding this so
called training montage.

       Raine
      You've apparently
      watched a whole bunch
         of them.
      Why don't you tell me.

Dante
That will all depend on
what kind of montage,
cara.
If, Rocky, I understand
you might be concerned
about your success rate.
But we can skip from 1
to 2.

I snorted, a smile threatening at my lips at him attempting
a joke. Not just attempting a joke, but attempting a joke in a
way that it was safe for me to react how I wanted. I didn't have
to worry about him seeing my reaction and what that might
give away to him.

  If Vampire Academy, I
  would like to see what it
  takes to convince you of
  it's worth.

       Raine
      I have no doubt you
      want it to be Vampire
        Academy.

Dante

Oh, was that not
obvious?
I didn't realise that was a
secret.

I mean, it was definitely the Vampire Academy kind of montage. Not that I was going to tell him that.

Raine

Exactly what did you
think was going to come
out of this conversation,
Dante?

Dante

A training montage,
nuvola :P

I didn't have to hide my smile at his boldness. I didn't have to pretend I didn't like the way he just came out and said what he wanted. I could totally sit there and let myself believe he might be completely sincere in his attentions. Just this once, I didn't have to be on alert. I didn't have to be looking over my shoulder. I was locked in my bedroom, but able to engage in carefully crafted banter with a guy who I could admit, when he wasn't there, made my heart race and my clit throb with nothing more than just existing.

Raine

You're not getting a
training montage.

Dante

Per favore, cara.

Raine

You know I don't

actually understand
Italian, right?

Dante

Si.

Why was that kind of adorable? Why was his defiance somewhat endearing? Why was I smiling more than I'd smiled in a whole year? And why couldn't I stop?

Raine
Voulez-vous coucher
avec moi?

Dante

Oui. Certainement. Le vôtre ou le mien?

Well, shit. That joke backfired.

Raine
How many languages do
you speak?!

Dante

7

Raine
Why?

Dante

We have international interests.

Raine
Is it a sex thing?
That how you seduce
Vanda?

I was unashamedly fishing for information on the two of them. I might have started the school year not caring if they fucked each other senseless multiple times a day. But I could

114

confess in the privacy of my own brain that I was slightly more invested in the answer now. And, annoyingly, more invested in the answer being quite specific.

Dante

:D Vanda and I have
never fucked. We have
not even kissed. She is
my friend.

I chastised myself for being relieved. I told myself there was no reason to be relieved. What did it matter to me if Vanda and Dante were…hooking up? Neither he nor I owed each other anything. That was between them… And yet… And yet, I was glad that the girl who had decided we were new best friends and the guy who effortlessly made my body come alive were just friends.

Raine

I'm sure I don't care.

Dante

Mm. I'm sure you don't.

Raine

Shouldn't you be
maiming someone or
something?
It is the middle of the
night.

Dante

If you want to know
what I'm doing, just ask.

Raine

…
I don't care what you're

doing.

I did.

Dante

I'm lying in bed thinking
of you.

Raine

Are you going to tell me
you've got your hands
down your pants? You
stroking it to the feeling
of your fingers buried
deep inside me?

Dante

I am now.

This was dangerous territory. Dangerous territory I wasn't
sure that I wanted to leave. I should, but I was oh so tempted
to see where this could go.

Raine

And if I told you I was
going to run my hand
over your cock?

Dante

You want to be in
charge, cara mia?
Prendilo.

Raine

Oh, Dante. You don't
want that.

Dante

Don't I? Why not?

Raine

Because once I've
touched and licked and
caressed every single
part of your body, I will
simply walk away and
leave you unfulfilled.

Dante

You kill me, cara.
Should I beg?

Raine

Try it and see where-
what it gets you ;)

Dante

I worship you.

Raine

Can you do it while I
sleep?

Dante

The consent there feels
incerto.
I bit my lip, a smile breaking free.

Raine

I meant I'm going to
bed.

Dante

Then I hope your
dreams are sweet.

Raine

You are a terrible mafia
brat.

Dante

:D Why do you say that?

Raine

Sweet dreams?

Worshipping me?

Anyone would think you

were soft for me.

Dante

I've told you, it's not

soft.

And I didn't realise mafia

brats were not allowed

fall in love.

Wait. What?

A squeak of surprise actually left my person.

Raine

Love?

Dante

We have emotions just

like your Elites, cara.

Raine

Pfft. I don't think the

Elites have emotions.

Dante

One more thing the

Immortali do better.

Raine

One more? That implies

there's anything else.

Dante

Oh, cara, there is so

much we do better.

> **Raine**
> I'm going to regret this,
> but what kind of things
> do you do better, then?

Dante
I thought you were
going to sleep?

> **Raine**
> You can't think of
> anything can you?

Dante
I can think of a lot of
things

> **Raine**
> Name one.
> Then I'll go to sleep.

Dante
Sex.

> **Raine**
> Really? How many Elites
> have you fucked to
> know that?

Dante
More than you, I'm sure.

That was an interesting admission. I wondered how Riker felt about that. I also wondered exactly how much better Dante really was and when he was going to convince me in person. Or rather, how long until I gave in and let him convince me in person.

Raine

And how exactly do you

do it better?

Dante

If you want to sleep,

sleep, cara.

Raine

Tell me this and I will.

Dante

An Immortale will not

rest until you cannot

take any more pleasure.

You will be their sole

focus. You are not to be

conquered, but adored.

It is a partnership.

Sacred.

Raine

No power play kinks?

Dante

Only when all parties get

off on it.

Yeah, okay. That sounded pretty sexy.

Raine

And on that note, I'm

going to sleep.

Dante

To dream of our power

play? ;)

I mean, our power play was also pretty sexy.

Raine

In your dreams, maybe.

Dante

Si. Every night.

Raine

Good night, Dante.

Dante

Buona notte, Raine.

Embarrassingly, I didn't put my phone down straight away. I searched social media for Dante and didn't actually go to sleep until I'd found a very attractive picture of him and brought myself to climax while imagining it was his fingers between my legs. God, he was so much better at it than me.

*

Class and my room were becoming the only safe havens I had left to me. I avoided the dining hall, and I didn't dare go to the library anymore. I couldn't risk West finding me. I was starting to drown under the anxiety of constantly wondering when he was going to come for me.

Even Dante's unrelenting presence – by my side whenever I was out of my room – wasn't enough to relax me. Although, the fact his presence was unrelenting was just another source of stress. I was becoming reliant on his protection and, the more reliant I was, the angrier I was. At him and me. At him for offering that protection and me for not stopping him, for letting him, for wanting him to.

I tried to tell myself I didn't need him. I didn't need anyone else. I was strong and ready to take my revenge myself, but I was acting like nothing more than that scared little girl who'd let them hurt her in the first place. And there was no way I was going to get my revenge if West still terrified me. After everything I'd done to live, to push through, to make myself the kind of person who could take that revenge on West, I was still falling short.

And Dante was both helping and hindering.

Him or Riker or Vanda, because if Dante wasn't with me then Riker or Vanda was. The Bishop was clearly displeased about being put on guard duty, but he did it with his bored scowl on his face and wielded his fists whenever he could. Meanwhile, Vanda was more than happy to pretend we were bonding, and I didn't have the energy to tell her we weren't.

But then, when I was taking refuge in my room, Dante's presence was in my texts and all the stress, that had eaten away at me all day, dissolved as we talked and bantered and joked. When we saw each other in person, neither of us mentioned our texts. I wanted to pretend there was nothing more between us than what the rest of the school saw, and he let me take the lead on that.

It was a few days later when Vanda was walking through the school with me. I didn't know where Dante was, but he was texting me. I hadn't seen Riker, so I assumed the two of them were doing what they counted as 'business' somewhere on campus.

"Did Dante tell you how much he enjoyed Vampire Academy?" Vanda asked me.

I managed to school my expression enough not to burst into laughter. "Not in…so many words," I said carefully.

She laughed, clear and bright. "What did he tell you?"

I snuck a sideways glance at her. "Oh, he didn't tell you?" I asked sarcastically.

She turned a smile on me. "Oh, he told me. I was just wondering if you would tell me."

"You're his friend, Vanda."

She inclined her head. "*Da*. I am." Her eyes shone and I

rolled my eyes.

"I didn't mean it like…" I shook my head. "Jesus," I muttered, and she laughed again.

"He flusters you."

"You fluster me."

She put her hand on her chest. "I'm flattered but, as we established, Dante is my friend and I would never do that to him."

"There is nothing between Dante and me."

She winked and nodded at me. "No. Of course not."

"There isn't. I don't owe Dante anything."

"*Net*. You don't. I do. And I know how he feels about you, so you are unfortunately off-limits."

"Unfortunately?" I asked, trying not to smile and encourage any of this bonding business.

"You don't think much of yourself, do you?" she asked casually.

My heart lurched. "What do you mean?"

She shrugged. "Your traumas have made you forget how amazing you are, haven't they?"

"What do you know about my traumas?"

"Very little. Dante keeps whatever he knows to himself. But I can extrapolate. You were here, dating West, happy and bright and healthy. Then you disappeared. Almost a year later, you return…changed. You will find you're not alone in the traumas created by this world."

I looked at her. "I was kind of hoping the Immortals treated their women better."

Her eyes were bright. "I don't doubt it and *you* have nothing to fear from the *Immortali*. Because for the most part, yes. But there are arseholes in every world and affiliation and society."

"You're implying Dante will save me. Why didn't he save

you, then?"

Her eyebrow rose. "Bold question, princess."

"You're the one who keeps telling me we're best friends now."

She grinned widely. "Dante did save me, but he also learned what happens if he hesitates."

I tried not to draw parallels. I tried not to wonder if that was why Dante was so aggressive about protecting me. Had he, once he'd made the decision to protect me, vowed he wouldn't hesitate again?

I was saved answering as I realised that Zak and Fletch were making straight for us. Zak pointed at me before drawing his hand across his throat, his step quickening as he walked towards me.

Vanda snorted. "These *idioty* think they can take us?"

I was obviously less certain about our abilities, but then I realised she didn't mean 'us' us. Because Riker and another Immortal appeared between us and Zak and Fletch. The other Immortal, who I only knew by sight – Franjo Sodan – was making for Zak, and Riker went for Fletch like it was personal.

I watched Riker's fist crash into Fletch's temple and even I winced. Even after everything, there was that small part of me that couldn't quite separate the Fletch being hurt now from the one I'd grown up with. From the one I'd loved. Because, whatever Fletch had let happen to me, I had loved him once. A part of me was having trouble remembering I didn't love him anymore. I'd separated West, for the most part, from who I'd spent so long thinking he was. But, in that moment, I couldn't do that with Fletch.

We'd been friends first. Before West. Before Lionswood and the hierarchy. It had been me and Fletch against the world. Two small souls in the vast universe, clinging to each other when we didn't have anyone else. He had been my rock. My best friend.

Then we'd arrived at Lionswood, and he'd gone and befriended West. West had filled a gap in Fletch's life that, no matter how hard I tried, I couldn't fill. But West had slowly gone from ignoring me to unable to keep his eyes off me. Or so I'd thought. So, I'd been told. West had chased me, and Fletch had vouched for him. I'd trusted Fletch when he said the rumours were just rumours. When he assured me that West was a good guy who was legitimately interested in me.

Against my wishes, I winced again as Riker's fist found its mark once more. Vanda's hand slipped into mine and I couldn't bring myself to pull away. I was going to take the comfort I was being offered in that moment, and I'd take it gladly.

Because, in front of me, was a very real reminder of everything I'd lost after the year before. Until that moment, I'd been glad I'd lost it. I'd been relieved that I was out. Fuelled by getting my revenge and leaving it all behind.

But here was the boy who held my hand when I skinned my knee. Who had shared his chocolates with me under the stairs at Christmas. Who had let me put my head in his shoulder during the scariest bits in a movie and hugged me even while he laughed.

West had taken so much from both of us, and Fletch had just…let him. Stood by and done nothing. Been complicit in West's atrocities through his silence.

Tears heated my eyes, and I found my hand tightening in Vanda's. She squeezed me back. Then she tugged on my hand and drew me away so I could fall apart in private.

I couldn't be sure but, based on the sight of the two of them later, Riker won the showdown. Fletch's eyes followed me at dinner, where Vanda kept me by her side, kicking every other Immortal off their table until Dante and Riker came in. Dante sat beside me, put his arm around my shoulder and kissed my temple, sending a glaring message to the rest of the school.

Vanda said something to him in Russian, to which he responded easily in kind.

Had I the energy, I would have stood up and left. As it was, I just sighed, "One day, you won't feel the need to talk about me behind my back." Then I amended, "In front of my back…?"

Dante's arm around me tightened comfortably and I leant into it. "Vanda was just telling me what happened."

I looked to Riker on the other side of the table. "He didn't tell you?"

"He couldn't tell me how you were."

"Novel idea, Dante. Just ask me."

"Would you tell me if I did?"

"You don't know if you don't ask."

He looked into my eyes. "How are you?"

"Fucking shit."

His face was neutral, but his eyes shone with warmth. "*Grazie*."

"For what?" I asked, recognising something.

"For telling me."

I shifted in my seat and went back to pushing my food around. "Don't get used to it."

Chapter Twelve

Of course, the one time I was alone, West was there and ready to give me shit. I just wasn't expecting the shit he had ready for me.

Some random kid walked past me first, a scowl on their face. "How could you?" they asked me, gone before I could clarify what in the hell I'd supposedly done now.

West stopped in front of me and pouted at me, but there was a shit-eating grin in his eyes. "Yes, Raine," he said sadly. "How *could* you?"

I frowned. "How could I what?"

"How could you leave me for Dante Wolfe?" His pout deepened and I was really tempted to slap it right off his face.

My eyes darted around. "Excuse me?"

He was playing the role of heartbroken, jilted, lovelorn teen to perfection. Everyone looking at him wouldn't even need to hear him to believe that he was mourning my loss.

"What did he promise you, sweetheart? What does he have on you? Let me save you from the big, bad wolf."

I took a step back and actually heard myself huff a humourless laugh. "Oh, my God. Seriously? You're not spreading that around the school, are you?"

He shrugged. "Of course, not! I don't spread rumours. Our private life – our love that you threw away for *him* – still means far more to me than that, even if you just disappeared and left me behind to pick up the pieces of my broken heart."

"I might throw up," I whispered.

"Morning sickness?" he sassed, and I frowned.

"Did you start that one as well?"

"How is our child, Raine? Who has him while you're here flaunting your infidelity in front of everyone? You would keep him from me?"

"Yeah, because Dante would want to be raising *your* child, you fucking idiot."

"He would if he thought it was his."

I rolled my eyes and did actually laugh now. "Wow. How many soaps are you watching, West? Have you taken up Romance writing? Small tip; less is more. There is such a thing as too many tropes and too many plots."

His lips twitched like he was going to snarl at me, but he kept the sad smile in place. "I gave you everything, Raine. You were my first love. I will never really get over you. I just wanted you to know that. Even if it doesn't change anything, I had to tell you."

"Right, while you're not getting over me, can you at least get over yourself? So, fucking dramatic," I muttered, looking him over and wondering how in the hell he got away with everything. How did people not see through his bullshit?"

West looked me over and I could see the venom in his eyes. I could see the anger and violence he was restraining. He knew that there were two ways to terrorise me: he could outright threaten me with physical violence or violation; or he could do what he was doing now. He could act like he would never harm me, so I wasn't going to know when it was coming. Because I wasn't so naïve as to think it was never coming.

Why the hell hadn't I stayed in my room?

"I'm not the one who accepted her loving boyfriend's

proposal then went and fucked Dante Wolfe."

"Oh, my God!" I cried, exasperated. "You are delusional if you think people are believing this narrative."

He shrugged again. "They don't need to believe it's one narrative, sweetheart. They just need to believe *one* of them is true. Once they believe one, they start to think the others *might* be true as well. They start to wonder *which* one is true, but don't doubt that one is. I mean, who leaves me for an Plutonis?"

"Me," actually popped out of my mouth, to the surprise of both me and West.

His eyes got dark and dangerous as he looked me over. "How long have you been fucking him, Raine?" he asked, his voice as dangerous as his eyes.

I swallowed, knowing I had to tow a fine line here. There was finding my spine around West and then there was pushing him to just kill me right here. "I know it's a foreign concept to you, West, but it is possible to defend someone below you without getting something in return."

"If you want to be below me, Raine, you know where to find me."

How did he always have a comeback! "I would like to see you below—" I stopped myself because I was about to add, 'six feet below'. He took my words the wrong way. Of course, he did.

"You want a ride, sweetheart?" His eyes scanned my body. "I could be persuaded."

Oh, I was…

I turned and walked away, fully believing he'd follow, but he didn't.

I'd had enough of this. I was holding my own and still not getting anywhere.

West oozed superior confidence from every pore, and he was too arrogant and cocky to stop and think that I wasn't falling for it. I don't think it had ever occurred to him that my defiance wasn't just me playing hard to get, but that I actually didn't believe the package anymore. That I wasn't impressed by the package anymore.

And the rumours he wasn't squashing!

Seriously? What in the hell did people think had happened to me? Did they think Dante had given me my scar in a fit of dominant rage? A rival affiliate to Dad's business empire?

I was so done. I was about three more mind-rants away from just texting my dad and telling him it was done. I was done. I had failed. I'd call in the air support and let him handle West's betrayal the way he'd wanted from the start. I'd totally prove myself unworthy of being his heir, of being mentored, and probably even loved. But I wouldn't have to deal with this shit anymore!

I burrowed into my blazer, mumbling rantings and obscenities to myself as I stormed for my room.

Dante fell into step with me from wherever he'd been that had kept him from my side. Which was a stupid thought! Because it wasn't like I wanted him by my side anyway! *Lies*.

Before he had a chance to open his mouth, I snapped, "I'm not in the mood. I'm going to my room. If you insist on annoying me, then it's going to have to happen there."

"Inviting me to your room, *cara*?" he teased.

I rolled my eyes. "Like you don't know exactly where it is. I wouldn't be surprised if you'd been in there before behind my back."

"As curious as I am to see a glimpse of what lies behind the curtain, I have not violated your privacy."

"No? Just my space, then?"

I felt like he was going to say something, but he held back. Instead, he just opened the dormitory door for me. I glared at him.

"I am capable of opening my own doors."

"Is it just *my* help you are so opposed to? Or everyone's?"

"Everyone's," I mumbled as I ducked inside. "Just ask my dad."

I felt rather than heard the rumble of his chuckle. "I think your father would get the wrong idea about us if I was to ask him to clarify."

My laughter was anything but humoured, and everything sarcastic and biting. "Haha. Ha. Because you're *so* against people getting the wrong idea about us, aren't you? You'd much rather the whole school *wasn't* convinced I dumped West for you!"

I unlocked my bedroom door and strode in, dumping my shoulder bag on the floor by my desk unceremoniously, and flopping onto my bed. I looked up and saw Dante hovering in the doorway.

My huff was slightly more humoured this time. "Suddenly scared of a girl's bedroom, Dante? I promise we don't bite. Hard."

Oops. That had not been the right thing to say. I mean, it had been very much the right thing to say, but it had Dante take a step into my room and close the door behind him. I heard the lock auto snap into place.

"Just because they kept you naive, *nuvola*, does not meant I haven't been in these dormitories *many* times before."

"Epic work, Dante," I sighed. "Get me alone in my room where *anything* could happen only to boast about your 'numerous' conquests. Excuse me while I rip my clothes off in a fit of sexual passion and beg you to add me to the inordinately long list of girls you now ignore."

He strode over to me and dropped between my legs to look up into my face. Damn, but he made a school uniform look good. He made anything look good. I bet he made naked look exceptional.

"Jealous, *cara*?" he teased, a gorgeous smirk hinting at those beautiful lips.

I took a breath and reminded myself I was stronger than my libido. "Why would I be jealous of girls who get to enjoy the one thing I want?" I sassed.

His eyes flashed bright, but his mouth pressed into a thin line. "You are in a mood today."

"I'm always in a mood around you, Dante. You bring out my natural snark."

The humour was back at his lips. "And I love it, but what are you so pissy about?" He inclined his head and amended, "Other than me, what are you so pissy about?"

"If I don't tell you, are you going to complain I'm shutting you out again?"

He smirked. "*Si*. If you really don't want to tell me, though, you don't have to."

Whether he was intentionally using reverse psychology on me or not, it was working. "I had a…conversation with West."

Dante took my hand. "Did he hurt you?"

"Not physically. Not this time."

I wanted to ask him where he'd been. Where was Riker? Vanda? Why had none of them been there for me? But how weak was that? To rely on others to save me. No one had come to save me last time. No one but that phoenix my imagination had created as some sort of comforting hero. The only person I could rely on was myself.

I slid my hand out of Dante's and tried to get a grip on

myself.

I'd promised myself I wouldn't be weak again. I wouldn't let anyone take advantage of me again. I wasn't sure anymore that Dante *was* going to take advantage of me. Not the way West had at least. But I could feel myself getting vulnerable around him. Our text chats had opened something in me. His touch opened something else. When it came to him, I may as well not have had any emotional armour at all.

Like he could feel the shift in me, Dante got up to sit beside me. "What did he do to you?" he asked, his voice soft and gentle.

I didn't look at him. "That would require him to touch me."

"He never touched you?"

"We never fucked. Since I've been back, I've started to think he can only get it up when it's non-consensual."

Dante might have been a lot of things, but stupid wasn't one of them. My eyes slid to him, and I saw he understood everything I was implying.

I chewed my lip, but it didn't stop me adding, "West personally never did more than kiss me." *That* implication hung heavy between us, and I didn't quite understand why Dante's reaction was so visceral.

His eyes darkened and I felt the anger sweeping off him in waves. "I'll kill him," he growled.

I swallowed hard. "No," I told him firmly and his eyes flashed with interest. "No. If anyone's going to kill West, it's going to be me."

His eyes were still dark as he looked me over, but there was something else in them. Something that called to me, that I wanted to respond to. It was biological, primal.

"Why are you looking at me like that?" I asked him, feeling ever so less assertive.

"I need– want to kiss you."

"You've never held back before."

Dante's fingers rested under my chin, and he made me look at him. "I am sorry our first kiss was not…" He took a breath. "That I took it without asking."

No. *No.* I was not going to get manic, warming, floaty heart flutters about Dante Wolfe. It wasn't happening.

I chewed my lip as I looked him over. His hand dropped from me as he searched my face. I couldn't tell what he was thinking. I wasn't sure I wanted to know, but curiosity got the better of me.

"It's not the only kiss you've taken without asking," I reminded him.

Darkness shadowed his eyes. This time as though he was pained. "After you kissed me, I *stupidamente* assumed they were not…unwelcome."

I nodded slowly. "I see."

"You have my apologies," he said.

I nodded again while I thought. Finally, my eyes found his again and, against what felt like better judgement, I said, "They're not unwelcome, Dante." I took my own breath to steal my nerves. "You can…stupidly assume until I tell you otherwise."

A triumphant humour lit his eyes, but the rest of his face was neutral. "Are you giving me permission to kiss you whenever I want?"

"I may not always be reciprocal. One day, I might tell you to never kiss me again. But, for now, I'm telling you that your kiss is not unwelcome. I might have been surprised, but not once has it been non-consensual." 'You are not West,' was what I wanted to add, because I knew that was where this was coming from; the idea that someone – even if not West – had touched me non-consensually and Dante not wanting to do that to me as well.

No. *No heart flutters.*

There went that cheeky half-smirk. "So, you are giving me permission?"

"I'm not giving you the satisfaction of saying those words, Dante. But…you're not wrong."

He leant one hand on the bed behind me as he trailed his fingers over my cheek. "Are you finally starting to believe you're mine, *cara*?" he teased.

I smirked. "I don't have to believe *anything* to get what I want from you, do I?"

He shook his head as he leant into me. "Not at all." His hand slid around the side of my neck, the tips of fingers tickling the line of my hair. He licked his lip sensually and slowly. "What do you want from me, *principessa*?" he purred, more begged.

I arched into him. "I think you know, Dante," I purred right back.

Heat blazed in his eyes, and he groaned. A real low, primal, needy sound that ignited my whole body. "Can you not say it, *nuvola*?"

"Can you not get it up unless I do?" I teased and he liked it.

Dante grinned at me as he pushed me down into the mattress. It was all feral and delicious. It was all craven promise and desire. His lips claimed mine as his fingers slipped into my pants. It was sheer luck that he was so single-minded. Sheer luck his hands didn't stray to the outsides of my legs. Sheer luck he didn't look down where my skirt had ridden up, exposing my legs because I'd found a ladder in my last pair of clean tights that morning.

Then, Dante's lips travelled down my neck as his finger

slipped into me and I stopped thinking about my legs. I stopped thinking about anything other than Dante Wolfe and the way he could play my body like he'd spent his whole life in the pursuit of mastering it.

"You like what I do to you, don't you, Raine?" he breathed as his lips brushed over my skin.

I nodded as my back arched off the bed.

I felt him smile against my jaw. "You're very quiet, *cara*," he teased.

"What do you want me to say?" I breathed.

"What do *you* want to say?" he asked.

"Honestly?"

"*Si.*"

"The only thing going through my brain right now…" I sucked in a breath as he slipped a second finger into me and his thumb brushed my clit. "…are various very breathy versions of your name, and…" I bit my lip as pleasure grew.

"And…?" he pressed.

"And," I said meaningfully, "Yes, Dante…right there."

He growled sexily as his teeth grazed over the sensitive skin of my neck, and the coil in me suddenly snapped. Hard and fast and sharp. My hands clawed at his back as I shoved my face into his shoulder to muffle my cry.

He slammed his fingers into me hard and deep, and my whole body arched into his as I moaned his name in one of those very breathy versions. I heard him chuckle, but his fingers didn't slow. His lips trailed over my neck and jaw and cheek and lips. He brought me to climax again quickly and easily, it breaking over me slower and deeper this time.

Then, I felt his fingers slow before he dragged them out of me. The backs grazed the inside of my thigh before he started sliding them over the top. My hand darted down and I took his hand, my fingers interlacing with his.

His eyes found mine and I wasn't sure what the surprise in his was about. My heart raced as we stared at each other, and both slowly sat up. I surreptitiously pulled my skirt back down, distracting him with a kiss as I did.

He opened his mouth, then the pocket against my leg started vibrating and his expression went wry.

"*Scusa*," he said, pressing another kiss to my lips as he pulled his phone out of his pocket and answered, "*Che cosa?*"

I heard Riker's voice through the speaker at Dante's ear as his lips were still roving over me as he listened. I couldn't understand the words but didn't know if I was too distracted or if it was Italian and my distraction made me not notice.

"Mm?" he answered at some point. "I could," he murmured. "What do you think?" More of Riker's muted voice. Dante smiled as his lips trailed over my cheek to my lips. "I am." Dante nodded. "Mm," he mumbled. "Fine. If I have to. *Ciao*."

He hung up, his lips still on me as he slipped his phone back in his pocket.

"You used English," I said as he looked at me.

The warm smile and...affection in his eyes deepened. "I did."

"Why?"

As he kissed me again, he said, "Because I have nothing to hide from you, Raine."

No. No heart flutters.

I took a breath and tried to get my heart under control. "But you have to go?"

He inclined his head. "*Si*. I'm sorry."

I shook my head. "You don't have to be sorry."

"I know I don't have to be," he said, his voice teasing. "But

I am."

No. Heart. Flutters.

"I suppose I'll see you later?"

"You will definitely see me later," he said, giving me one more kiss before he started to stand up.

For some reason, I wrapped my hand around his tie and brought him back for one last kiss, again feeling him smile against me.

"Sorry to see me go, *cara*?" he asked, his eyes sparkling.

"Sorry I won't get to take what I want from you for the rest of the night," I teased right back.

He chuckled. "*Bene*. I will be back if I can, then."

I bit my lip and I saw in his eyes that he knew I was hiding a smile. I gave a coy shrug that we both knew was a front. "It doesn't bother me."

Another rough chuckle that I felt shoot right through me. "Of course, not. *Ciao*."

"Bye."

Dante didn't make it back that night, but he did text me. Not just to let me know he couldn't come back, but also to offer me a very visual description of what he would have done to me had he been able to make it back. It was almost just as good as if he had.

Chapter Thirteen

One morning, there was a knock on my door and panic chilled my blood.

In the weeks I'd been back, no one had knocked on my door. Until now, it hadn't occurred to me that no one had ever bothered me in my room. The bathroom, yes. But not my bedroom. That was concerning. Or perhaps just coincidental?

They knocked again. Two short, hard raps.

My heart thundered as I walked over to the door. It was locked, but I hadn't noticed anyone trying the handle or anything, so who in the hell would come to my door and actually knock? I was on alert, but doubted that West or anyone else was going to be knocking; I'm sure they'd just break it down or wait for me to come out before jumping me.

I wrenched it open before I either lost my nerve or they decided to knock again. My heart's thundering skipped one, two, three beats as I took in the sight in front of me. Heat pooled deep in me, and I pretended I have no idea what he was doing there. Or why.

Dante had backed up to the other side of the hall as I opened the door so I had full view of him in a pair of black tracksuit pants, black runners, and a sleeveless hoodie, the hood pulled up over his hair, but it still peeked out over his forehead in a jagged V. His golden eyes shone in the semi-dark of the hall.

The muscles of his arms twitched as he shifted on his feet,

the tattoos rippling in a way that made me want to run my hands – or my tongue – over them. I wanted to trace the outline of every single swirl and cross and skull and see what treasure awaited at the end of them.

"What are you doing here, Dante?" I asked, as though it wasn't painfully obvious.

He cracked his knuckles. "You seem like you need a run."

I chewed on my lip because I wasn't sure what my reaction would have been otherwise. I didn't trust what I might do or say if I didn't take a second to use my big brain. He was savvy enough to have realised that I ran for solace. He'd noticed I'd stopped running. He'd seen I had very little solace. He'd probably even guessed that I only wasn't running because I was scared West and not Dante would be the one to follow me. And he was giving me a way to run without following me.

Together.

Not owned.

"Won't you be cold?" I asked, my eyes darting to his arms again.

He flexed his biceps and I told myself I didn't care for it. "I've seen you run, *nuvola*. At your pace, I'll keep warm." He looked down, then snuck a look up at me through his eyelashes with the sexiest half-smirk at his lips. "Unless you're offering to keep me warm some other way?"

To say it wasn't tempting would have been a lie. And I'd already lied to myself a dozen times just since I'd opened the door. So, I wouldn't deny the entire visual was tempting. I could just drag him into my room and find solace in a whole new way. But my legs burned, and it sent a lance of pain to my heart, like my anguish was reminding me he'd just walk away if he saw them. I'd been lucky so far that he hadn't. Too lucky. So, no matter how much my clit throbbed for his touch, a run was going to have to suffice.

I looked him over once more, as though not at all bothered by the glorious package in front of me. "I'll get changed."

He nodded and took a step back to lean on the wall behind him. I paused, surprised he hadn't tried coming in under the guise of making sure there wasn't anyone hiding in my wardrobe or something ridiculous. His eyebrow cocked like he saw my surprise and was amused by it, like he was saying 'do you *want* me to come in?' I swallowed hard and disappeared into my room.

He was on the phone when I walked back out, rapid Italian flowing to whoever was on the other end. He didn't sound particularly agitated, but short. Like he wanted the conversation over as soon as possible.

"*No,*" he said with a warm chuckle. "*Lei mi batterà. Facilmente.*" A pause and another, bigger laugh. "*Non sono frustato. Lei è mia. Certo. Dopo. Ciao, vecchio.*"

He slipped his phone into his pocket and turned to me, his laugh still on his face in the shape of a brilliant smile that utterly blew me away. My heart tingled. My stomach fluttered. I had to lick my lip because there was something else I wanted to do with it. He really was devastatingly gorgeous. Even more so when he looked at me the way he was looking at me now; soft smile on his face, his eyes open and warm and bright.

That spark shone deep inside me. I could feel its warmth, drawing strength from his. It was both horribly addictive and terrifying. Forgotten and foreign… And yet, so familiar. Like I'd once looked into a lamp and now I was faced with a bright and shining star. Something so far away, but reaching through the darkness, offering a source of light.

I stamped out the spark and pushed away the feelings battering at me.

"If you have…business to attend to…?" I offered.

His smile widened again, and his eyes sparkled. My heart lurched in my chest. Like it was trying to get to him. "I do not."

I nodded slowly, not sure what to say to him for once. "Riker?"

He inclined his head. "*Si.*"

Another wanky nod from me. "Cool."

He gave a rough huff of laughter. "You are not one for small talk, *nuvola*. Nervous you can't keep up with me?"

I felt myself rise to his challenge. "Nervous I'll get too far ahead, maybe." The insult was there, but the attached sentiment was the totally wrong message. Not a lie, but not something I wanted him to know.

He smirked. "*Ovviamente.*"

Still knowing absolutely nothing about Italian, I could only incline my head. "Shall we?"

"Lead the way, *cara.*"

I had my hair up, and I forced my back to stay straight as we walked to the running tracks. People watched and whispered as we passed, and I was sure I could guess what most of them were saying. Dante and I in workout gear, heading for the woods. We either had some very specific kinks, or we were doing something somewhat domestic together.

Dante walked beside me, and I felt his fingers brush against mine. It was the sort of support and empathy that Vanda had shown me the other day. That 'I'm here for you if you need me' kind of motion that was threatening to undo me in front of all these people.

So, as soon as we hit the tracks, I launched into a steady jog. I hadn't had time to warm up properly, so I was just going to have to start out slowly. Dante kept up with me no problem. We jogged in blessed quiet, the only sound our feet and our breaths.

Just as I decided I was warm enough to put on a burst of speed, he decided to show off. He turned to jog backwards, throwing me a cocky, sexy, cheeky grin. Then I lurched past him, and with an "eh!" he scrambled to turn back around and follow. But his foot caught a branch and he fell with a heavy Italian curse.

I stopped and looked back at him, feeling the laughter bubbling up inside me. He was muttering to himself in Italian as he sat up and stretched himself out. Then he turned to look at me and saw me barely containing my laughter. A smile tugged on the corner of his lips, and I was in danger of losing the battle. I tried to look away from him, but my eyes kept sliding back. The smile on his face grew and grew. I had to bite my lip hard to stop myself. Then, finally, neither of us could contain it and we both barked out a loud laugh that startled a bird in a nearby tree.

I walked back to him and held my hands out to help him up.

He took them, a heat curling through eyes that pinned mine as he got to his feet.

"Try avoiding the obstacles," I suggested.

"*No, davvero?*" he said, and I heard the heavy, humoured sarcasm in his playful voice. "I would not have thought of that."

"Try and keep up, Dante," I said, with a wink and took off again.

He swore again, then followed. And now we were moving at a better pace, he had trouble keeping up. Where I leaped over roots and branches from plenty of practice, he was far less fluid. Not that I let him fall too far behind.

I paused to catch my breath and wait for him to catch up.

When he finally did, I was gratified to see he was breathing far more heavily than I was.

"Cardio not your strong suit?" I teased and he grinned.

"Tease me more, *principessa*, and I might demand we do this more often."

A thrill ran through me at the implication that he wasn't just turned on by the shit I gave him, but he enjoyed it on a level that wasn't just sexual. "I don't know. I'd hate to leave you behind."

"Practise makes perfect, *cara*," he said. "And I will suffer any number of humiliations and minor bruising to see you like this."

Everything in me clenched and twinged and tingled. "Like what?" I asked, aiming for flippant.

"The most relaxed I have ever seen you. The happiest. I don't think I have ever seen you really laugh."

The tongue that swept over my lip this time was nervous. "I laughed all the time before."

He shook his head. "Not like this. Not like you meant it. Not like you weren't looking over your shoulder." God, his voice was... Need and want and undeniable greed. I saw the sentiment mirrored in his eyes. "I want you to always feel like that."

That connection swirled between us, and I felt my feet take a step towards him. He took a step towards me. My whole being cried out for him, for the way he made me feel. I loved it, but I also hated it.

I was swiftly becoming dependent on Dante. I craved the attention he unhesitatingly lavished on me, but there was something about it that felt dirty. Like I was cheating. Not on West because he'd lost his claim over me when he'd let them hurt me, when he'd hurt me, and by wanting to hurt me every single day since he'd finally noticed I'd returned. No, it felt like I was cheating on me. On the semblance of life that I'd clawed back for myself. On the revenge that kept me breathing every day.

But then there was Dante, looking at me like I had the potential be the most precious thing in the world. Like he didn't even know he was giving it away. Even West, for all his carefully crafted looks and actions in winning me, had never looked at me with such sincere…longing.

And it was a longing that I felt anchored in me for the man in front of me.

Like maybe he *was* that pinpoint of light in a universe of darkness.

As stupid as I wanted to tell myself that was, I wanted to give into it. Even just for now. I could go back to pretending I didn't want or need him later. For now, I just needed to…

We crashed together in the middle of the woods, our arms wrapping around each other as our lips met in a frenzy. My fingers got caught in his hood, where it had long since fallen around his neck, and found their way to his hair. His slid to grip my hips tightly as he groaned against my mouth, sending a jolt of need straight to my clit.

One of my hands slid down his chest and tightened around a fist of his hoody near his hip. His fingers tightened further, and my goosebumps chased each other across my body, making my nipple pinch.

We took a few stumbled steps backwards until I felt a tree at my back. Dante put his hand behind my head like he thought that would protect it, making his arm wind around me in such a comforting way. His other hand was still on my hip and his thumb brushed over my pelvic bone. My hips bucked against him, and I felt him smile.

He gave me what he knew I wanted. His fingers trailed up to the waistband of my leggings and, despite the no doubt awkward angle, slipped under and straight to my clit. I breathed against him in pleasure. His touch was like fire and lightning. It made my breath catch, my heart skip, and fostered such a deep-seated hunger in me I knew only he would ever be able to sate.

One finger slid into me. Two. And that knot of pleasure wound tighter and tighter in me. Dante held me on that precipice expertly while I waited for the coil to snap. I nipped his lip playfully and he answered with not just a smile, but by pressing his thumb to my clit and – snap – pleasure crashed over me in a heavy wave.

My fingers fisted in his hair as I tensed around him. His hands slowed as he drew my climax out as long as possible. I was still breathing hard as my hands started for the top of Dante's trackpants. There was no sense of victory or triumph in him to make me pause, but I still paused.

My mind ran at a million miles a minute, but I caught every thought.

The way Dante touched me like it – I – meant something to him. Like my pleasure and safety were his sole concern. The way he never, not once, left me to West if he could help it. That he would go to war against West for me, even while he was waging war with his Bishop over me as well. That he told me I was his. That he clearly wanted me and knew I wanted him.

If he *was* sincere about me being his – and I wasn't sure yet whether he was – then he could work for it, damn it. I wasn't just going to give it up and have him decide he was done. Dante was one of the only things keeping West from stomping me into the ground. Dante was also one of the only things keeping me from stomping myself into the ground. He provided protection but also solace, as much as I hated to admit it.

I knew Lords could lie as well, if not better, than Kings. So, if Dante really was serious and he really wanted to convince me that I was his, then yeah, he was going to have to work for it. It didn't hurt that him working for it was the same as me getting plenty of pleasure. Pleasure that Dante was clearly very happy to give while getting nothing back.

It was a bit obvious that I'd started reaching for his trousers, then stopped, but Dante did nothing more than bring me to climax once more before we finally pulled apart and headed back to school.

*

I was feeling weird about our run that morning. Invigorated and more relaxed than I had since I'd come back to Lionswood, but weird. I felt like we'd crossed an invisible border in our relationship, such as it was, and a huge brick wall had slammed up in place behind us meaning there was no way to backtrack.

So, I wasn't watching where I was going as I wandered the library late that night. I'd stupidly assumed no one knew I was in there. I even more stupidly assumed that everyone else would be partying the night before going home for the Autumn holidays, not worrying about loners in the library.

But of course, there was one guy who was thinking about loners in the library. One specific loner in the library.

I felt a hand close over my mouth as my arm was pulled behind my back.

"No funny business this time, sweetheart," West growled in my ear.

Gone was the playful, if menacing, teasing.

"Time to see what all the fuss is about," he snarled.

He grabbed a handful of my hair and hauled me over to a table to shove me face first into it. His hand came off my mouth, but I was too stunned and panicked to scream anymore. He was half bent over me, his arm holding me down.

I felt him fiddling with his trousers at my back and I didn't have to imagine what was coming. I thrashed against him, but he was ready for me to fight back this time. The vibration of his laughter rumbled through my back, and it chilled my blood.

Then his hands were at my waistband and tugging on it. I couldn't believe I was letting this happen again. Worse yet, I couldn't believe this was happening again and my first instinct was that I wasn't just letting myself down, but Dante as well. What the fuck did I owe him?

Strength, a little voice in my head suggested.

Dante's presence, annoyance, protection, banter. It had all fostered strength in me since I'd come back. Boldness. Belief in myself. It gave me an outlet to practice being the person I wanted to be. I hadn't been left isolated and lonely, to merely wallow and languish in the prison I'd made for myself.

"West, don't do this," I begged.

"Why not, Raine? Because you don't want me to?" he teased. "Oh, it's sweet you think you have a say."

I gritted my teeth while I thought about how best to get out of this. West's much more significant weight had me pinned. I didn't have my knife anyway so I was losing this either way. The only thing left to me was words. "You're smarter than this, West."

He leant his lips to my ear. "I'm smart enough to get away with it."

"Don't. Do. This," I tried one more time.

He didn't have a chance to respond.

"*Lei ha detto no*," came the very low, dangerous voice behind us. I felt West tense as a pleasant thrill ran through me, even despite the complicated onslaught of emotions that hit me.

Then West was gone from my back, and I turned to find Death himself facing him. Dante was livid. Fucking livid. I'd never seen anyone as angry – an incarnation of pure fury – as Dante looked just then.

He breathed so heavily, the arms at his sides rose and fell with each one.

West had the fucking audacity to grin at Dante. "Do I interrupt when *you're* with her?" he asked, all charm and superiority. "Wait your turn and I'll share her with you."

"She is not yours," Dante growled, his lips barely moving.

West actually laughed. "I think it's safe to say the same to you."

Dante took a step towards him, and West lost a bit of his cocky preening. "Walk the fuck away, little King."

"Why don't you make me?" West goaded him. "Go on. I know you're dying to hit me. I touched her after all. And look, I'm not dead. Are you weak, Wolfe? A weak little pup. All bark. No bite."

Dante was shaking with anger, and I had to hand it to West because I would *not* have been going at Dante right then. I was surprised that Dante hadn't just straight out killed him already.

"No? Not going to follow through on your threats?" West pursed his lips like he was disappointed. "Shame. All right, then. I'll tell you what we'll do. You can have her tonight. You can have her all holidays for all I care. Giving her time to relax her defences is going to make it so much more enjoyable when I break through them, anyway."

Forget Dante's fury. *I* was pissed!

I stood up straighter, but may as well have faded into the background for all the cares West gave about my indignation. He just threw Dante a coquettish wave and sauntered away, leaving me and Dante standing in the library together.

Once he was sure West was gone, Dante hurried over to me.

I was still watching the direction West had left, anger in me mounting from every conceivable direction.

"Are you okay?" Dante asked, his hand reaching for me.

Unthinkingly, unhesitatingly, I whirled on him and smacked him in the face. He glared at me in return.

"That is the thanks I get?"

He shouldn't need thanks in the first place. First, he worms past my defences, he makes me…feel things, and now West? My heart was beating so hard that, through the cascade of falling, crashing, tumbling thoughts, I wondered if I was having a coronary. But I recognised this feeling; panic attack. A panic attack fuelled by too many emotions that I didn't want to feel ever again.

It hurt, just thinking about them. And now I could feel them pushing up against the barrage of thoughts my mind was hiding inside. They raged and ranted and railed against the barricade my mind had thrown up, and they were finding their way in.

Fear.

Pain.

Danger.

…Run.

But more.

Warmth.

Light.

Safety.

The answering feeling was still the same.

…Run.

My breathing was so ragged and heavy, I was close to hyperventilating, and I took a step back from Dante.

"Don't you ever…" I snarled. "Ever do that again."

He was understandably confused, but reason had distinctly left the building and I was at DEFCON 1. Everything around me had to burn. Especially me.

"What?" he breathed.

"I don't need your help, Dante. I don't want your help. Okay? It's *unwelcome*," I spat at him, and I saw his eyes widen in understanding.

"He was going to–"

"And it's not your job to save me!" I yelled at him.

He took a step back. "Raine?"

I shook my head. "I don't know what sin you think 'saving' me is going to erase from your past, Dante. But I'm not yours. I never have been. I never will be. This game? It's done. I wish I could say it was fun while it lasted." *Lies.* "I save myself."

"You will die." It wasn't a threat. It was a warning. A plea.

A ghost of a smirk lit my face. "Then I'll die."

His jaw clenched. "That's it?" he clarified, and I nodded. "The game is done. You want me to back off?"

"I want you to back off. I want you to go back to ignoring my existence the same way you did before I came back. I never mattered to you before then anyway, so I don't see why I'd matter now."

He stiffened. Something about my words apparently hit a nerve and, for one brief millisecond, I regretted my hastiness. Then he nodded and my decision was sealed. "*Bene*. West can have you, then. I will not step in again. Unless you ask."

I bristled. "Good. And I won't ask."

His smirk was all predatory. "Just know that *when* you do, *principessa*, my help will not come for free next time."

I opened my mouth to argue with him further, but he'd turned and was walking away. Which was probably a good thing, because I had nothing remotely witty or scathing on the tip of my tongue. I watched him go and…

And the reality of what I'd just done hit me.

Dread settled in my stomach, and I actually doubled over the carpet and dry retched.

"You fucking idiot," I muttered to myself.

Sorrow joined the dread as I sank to the carpet and leant against the leg of the table.

I felt this hollowness inside me that wasn't just in watching Dante walk out of my life, but in knowing that I was truly alone again. Alone and utterly powerless.

Because, for all my training – for all my planning – my power was still zero.

I could protect myself if any of them came for me again – in theory – but even were I to get the upper hand and manage to give West a beating, it would do nothing. I'd get worse in return. Death didn't scare me, but dying unavenged terrified me.

No. If I was going to ruin West, I really couldn't do it alone. Because I needed to pull him down to nothing. Systematically destroy everything that gave him power. Even killing him wouldn't be enough. I needed to raze his kingdom to the ground.

But who in this place full of assassins and dealers and savvy entrepreneurs was going to help me? Everyone either feared or revered the Elites.

Everyone but the Immortals.

The only reason the Immortals didn't rule the school was because they had no interest in kingdoms or empires. They were tight-knit. Exclusive. Uninterested in wielding power over the world. All they wanted was to keep people out of their business and let them get on with what they did best.

After this, their help would not be guaranteed. Not the kind of help I needed to really destroy West.

Then again, perhaps the Lord who'd stolen more than a few kisses would still be willing to help me bring his nemesis to his knees. Even if he'd already tried and I'd thrown it back in his face. I certainly didn't lose anything by asking. Nothing but my pride – but I didn't have much of that left, really – and whatever price he claimed.

I'd learnt a lot from my father since I left Lionswood. If I couldn't persuade Dante to help me after I'd spent all term telling him I didn't want his help, then my father was right, and I really wasn't worthy to be the heir to the Edwards estate.

Chapter Fourteen

It was the end of the holidays and I had relished my week of semi-loneliness. At least as much as Dante had been willing to give me with the rest of the school – and his 'official' protection – gone.

I'd resisted his help until now, but I could acknowledge now that there was no way I was going to be able to finish my mission without accepting it. Not just passively letting him help, but actually asking him to actively help me after all-but spitting in his face. He knew more about revenge and pain and torture than I did, as much as I'd tried to educate myself.

So, I walked up to the foreboding spire that was the *Torre Degli Immortali*. It was a tall, circular turret tucked away in the edge of the woods, towards the back of the school. There were no lights outside it, and I always thought it would be fun trying to get to it without the light of the moon to guide you.

Honestly, I didn't expect to see many people. No one would be back until the next day, because no one in their right mind missed the Lionswood Academy Halloween party. The fact that the next term started the day after it was just coincidental.

And I didn't see many people. In fact, I didn't see any people.

I pushed the heavy wooden door open and shivered as I stepped inside. It was barely warmer in there than the air outside, which felt like it was getting colder every day.

The ground floor was all stone with a staircase disappearing up into the darkness above. Wooden doors stood to the side, and I wondered where they led. Where did I go? How did I find Dante in all this? There must have been at least six floors with who knew how many bed- and other rooms. What was I going to do? Check them all until I found him?

"Trespassers will be more than prosecuted, little princess," came a voice.

I looked up and saw Riker gliding down the stairs. His eyes were firmly locked on me, and I was sure he could have a blade in me before I could plead my case. Lucky for me, Riker was more loyal to his lord than any of the Elites were to West. And he knew Dante would shred him to ribbons if he touched me.

There were some perks to being marked by the Lord of the Immortals.

"I'm looking for Dante," I told him.

"What makes you think he's here?" Riker asked, his voice low and bored and dismissive.

"I know he's here, Riker."

"Really? Usually, he's staked out outside your room."

I frowned as Riker started walking across the floor to me. "I'm sure I've seen you there more often than him."

"He has many demands on his time. That is why he has me and the *Immortali*."

I nodded, suddenly feeling like maybe I owed him something. "I appreciate it."

Riker shrugged. "I couldn't care less. Dante Wolfe orders it and I obey."

I had a feeling there was more to it than just ingrained loyalty. Not that Riker – or any of the Immortals – would ever admit it; that they actually liked Dante. Not the way you like your friends, as if I knew what that was like. But the way you legitimately respect someone, you care about the things they care about, and you would do anything for them the way you knew they'd do anything for you.

Of course, that was all conjecture on my part. I'd never experienced any of those things, nor really seen it. Not until Dante marked me and I couldn't help but see more of the Immortals than anyone needed or wanted to.

"Well, I need to see him," I said. Preferably before I lost my nerve.

Riker leant against the pillar in the middle of the room. "What about?"

"None of your concern," I told him, forcing my strongest and most authoritative voice.

An amused twitch lit his face for but a moment. "And the kitten gets claws," he said with a wry scoff. "Am I meant to be impressed?"

"Oddly," I said with a sarcasm if my own, "I don't really care what you think of me."

Well, that hadn't been the right thing to say.

Riker drew himself up and stepped into my space. My heart thudded in my chest, but I refused to be that scared little girl again. I wasn't here to ask the Lord of the Immortals for help to be that scared little girl ever again.

"You're mighty disrespectful for someone who's come into our house and wants an audience with our lord."

"He's your lord, not mine."

The corner of Riker's lip rose in a snarl. "Didn't the little boy king teach you any manners?"

My hand flew out of its own accord and slapped him across the face; there was no way I could punch him properly at that angle. His head whipped sideways, but I saw the scowl before he slowly turned it full onto me.

"Dante might find that shit a turn on, but you ever raise a hand to me again and, orders or no, Dean's policy or no, I will end you and your little Elite friends," he growled sending a skittering of panic up my spine.

I held my own. "They're not my friends."

"Then you won't want to spend eternity in the same shallow grave." I could tell he didn't believe me.

Honestly, why would I go to the bother of this whole charade just to – what? – bring the Immortals down? The Elites hated the Immortals, but none of them would stoop to physical disfigurement and the shit I'd been through, before and after my ten-month absence, just to try and get any kind of leg up on them.

"If I was working with them, I would have let Dante fuck me by now," I told Riker.

He still didn't look convinced. "Just give me a reason," he begged in a whisper, and he closed in on me. "Just give me a reason and I'll put us all out of your misery."

"I'll keep that in mind," I answered, sarcastically chipper. "I just have one super important thing I need to do, then I'll take you up on your offer."

A flicker of surprise and question crossed his face. Then he asked, "What do you need to do?"

"None of your business." I paused for dramatic effect. "But it *is* your lord's business."

He sniffed as he looked me over, like just looking at me could tell him if I was lying or not. "Fine," he finally said. "Follow me."

Riker led me through a door, and I realised that the Immortals took their hierarchy seriously. Far more seriously than the Elites. The Elites had done everything to fit into a modern world. The Immortals had no need.

The room was dark grey stone, cold emanating from the walls. There were crests and portraits and busts around the edge of it. Just looking at them, I could tell that they went back a long way. Hundreds of years long. The Immortals were an institution older than Lionswood itself. Older than the Elites. They were the shadow rulers of this whole thing.

The rest of the room was bare. Not even a rug on the floor. At the end, was a raised dais. And on that dais…

Dante didn't just wield power and command respect by simply existing, he also did it from a throne. An actual fucking throne.

"Raine Edwards," he said, his voice echoing in the empty room. "What pleasure brings you to me this day?"

"Dramatic, much?" I huffed as I walked towards him.

Dante had one ankle on a knee, his elbow on the arm rest with his chin on his fist as he looked me over. "You came to me, *cara*," he reminded me. "You came into my house. You will follow our protocols."

"Will I?" I asked, my eyes sliding to Riker, who leant against the wall to my left with his arms crossed expectantly.

Riker smirked, no doubt thinking I was going to get my comeuppance. Both of them knew I was here for something. For all our weeks of flirting and…more, I had never set foot anywhere near the Tower. The only reason I would actively seek Dante out in his home would be because I wanted something. And Riker was just waiting for me to be brought down a notch.

"As much as it pleases me to see you, *principessa*," Dante said, bringing my attention back to him. "I have many obligations. If there is something you…need, then say so."

I frowned at him. I was about five seconds away from just walking back out and not bothering about it. Maybe I could give up my mission of revenge and just put myself out of everyone's misery. I was sure I could come to grips with that. Besides, once I was gone, I wouldn't care about West or Dante or revenge anymore. No, that was actually sounding mighty appealing.

But Dante leaned forward and licked his lips sensually as his eyes scanned my face. His smirk was knowing, it was teasing, it was a dare. 'Ask me', it begged. That stupid spark of something flared in me and survival instincts kicked in.

"Help me destroy West," I said. I didn't beg. It wasn't a question. It was as polite an order as I felt he deserved.

Dante scoffed as he leant back again. "*Destroy* the little king? I cannot see any reason why I'd want to do that."

"He's your closest rival. I'd have thought you'd enjoy the challenge."

"I can protect you without destroying him."

"I won't take protection without destruction."

For a moment, he looked like he was about to give in, then he smirked. "What you fail to realise, *piccola nuvola*, is that I already have West where I want him–"

"Even if you could have him under your boot?"

His smirk widened. "I'm quite *contento* with the status quo. I get rid of the puny king, and another merely rises in his place. West is weak. I can manage West. Who says the next king of the Elites is someone so…biddable?"

"What if it was a queen?"

I felt Riker's attention pique, but he said nothing.

Dante's smirk dropped and his eyebrow rose. "A queen?"

I nodded. "What if it was me?"

The smirk returned, but softer. He was intrigued. "You?"

"You don't think I'm strong enough?"

He shook his head. "I didn't say that. I doubt you think

you're strong enough, but I know you'd handle it."

That surprised me. "Why?"

"Because you…*handle* me."

There was so much in those last two words. The suggestion of exactly what I could handle. The surety I wouldn't disappoint. The desire to handle me right back. The promise of how deliciously sinful and decadent we would be together.

But now wasn't the time to be thinking with my smaller head.

"That doesn't mean I'd be biddable," I said quickly.

The humour reached his eyes, and he licked his bottom lip. "I beg to differ."

"You'd have to beg, I promise."

The challenge was in his eyes, but I didn't know which way he'd turn. The Lord of the Immortals was just as likely to agree as he was to throw me out the top window of his Tower for boring him with the trivialities of my life, no matter what he claimed I was to him.

"You want my help destroying West?" he clarified.

I nodded. Begrudgingly. "I can't do it alone," I admitted through gritted teeth.

"And why ask me?"

"Because…" *You flirt with me. You kissed me. You make me feel something more than pain and vengeance for the first time in a long time and I want to be around it as much as possible.* No, that's stupid. Horniness was no reason to hang out with Dante Wolfe. "…you're the only one who will."

"Why is that?"

I knew he was baiting me. If it got me the help I needed, then I was relatively comfortable rising to it. "You're the only one with as much contempt, disgust, disregard, and dislike for him as me."

He huffed a rough laugh and scratched his ear. "*Vedo*. One would think, then, if I'm your only option, that you'd be a bit more…respectful in your request."

I straightened my back. "I'll get your help any way I damned well please," I snapped.

The flash of emotions across his face was intoxicating. Disbelief. Annoyance. Amusement. Respect. Desire.

"No. You'll get my help any way *I* damned well please," he said slowly.

"Does that mean you will help?"

"You wanted to play the game, *cara*?" He ran his tongue over his bottom lip and nodded. "I will help. For a price."

Unsurprising. I'd told him on numerous occasions he was no knight in shining armour, and he'd warned me he wouldn't agree to help me without asking something in return. So, I thought about that. My father would no doubt bankroll whatever Dante asked. "How much do you want?"

"Oh," he laughed. "I don't want money, *principessa*. That's too easy."

I swallowed. Hard. "What do you want?"

He leant towards me. "*Tre favori*. Three favours. Call them…wishes, if you like."

"Wishes?" I scoffed, attempting to keep it cool. "You want three wishes?"

He nodded. "Yes, I do."

"And what are they?"

"Undisclosed. Promised. Irrefusable. To be called if and when I so please."

I was starting to rethink the sense in coming to Dante for help. Who knew what favours he'd call, or when? Was my revenge worth whatever his twisted mind could think up?

"And if I did refuse?"

"Deal is off, and all my powers of destruction will be focussed on you."

Look, that was fair. The way I now knew our world worked, that was fair. "Okay…" I said slowly.

He was hiding just how excited he was at the idea, but I saw it in his eyes. "You agree to my terms?"

I almost shook my head. "I'm considering your terms. Can I think about it?"

"Of course. Shrewd heads never agree to a business arrangement on the spot."

"A business arrangement?"

"What else is this?"

"Fine. I suppose you want a contract with that as well?"

A wicked glee filled his eyes. "You do know the way to a depraved soul's heart."

Takes one to know one, I thought.

I nodded. "Fine. I'll think about it and let you know."

He inclined his head.

As I turned to walk away, he called, "The deal runs out at midnight at the Halloween party. If you don't find me by then, you're on your own."

I turned back to him. "I'm not going to the Halloween party."

"You are if you want my help."

I opened my mouth and closed it a few times, not quite sure what to say.

His crooked smile told me exactly what he was thinking of doing with my mouth.

"I don't have a costume," I said, rather feebly.

He shrugged. "That seems like a you problem."

"You're the one making me go."

"You want it to be an us problem? You just have to agree

to my terms."

"There will never be an us," I told him as I started to walk away again.

He nodded, but like he totally didn't believe me. "I'll see you tomorrow night, *nuvola*," he called after me.

His next words were said so quietly I almost didn't hear him. By the time I'd registered what he'd said and turned around, he was gone, his words still echoing in my head.

"If you can find me…"

Chapter Fifteen

Trust Dante Wolfe to make everything in my life difficult.

I'd done as he'd instructed. It hadn't been easy to find a costume on such short notice, but I'd become adept at moving in shadow and getting unseen into places I wasn't supposed to be. So, I'd raided the attic of the Coxwright Manor, the home of the Elites, and found an old wedding dress and veil. I'd been in the maintenance buildings and found some red paint. I'd been in the woods and hunted down some walnuts. I'd even lost enough weight to the point it was going to suit my costume perfectly.

Gothic zombie bride wasn't exactly sexy, but then I didn't give a shit.

I didn't even really know why I'd gone to such lengths because I still wasn't convinced that I was going to agree to Dante's terms. Three undisclosed wishes to be called at *any* time? What were we? Living in some ridiculous farce of a fairy horror tale?

So, not only had I gone to great pains to get a fucking costume, but I was currently going through great pains just to fucking find him. Because, unsurprisingly, he was playing hard to get. Part of me didn't blame him. In many ways, it could be said that I'd been playing hard to get all term. He'd literally begged me to let him help me, I'd thrown it in his face, then had the audacity to ask him for his help.

I couldn't find him anywhere. I kept thinking I saw him out of the corner of my eye – felt him – but by the time I turned, he was definitely not there.

Happily, no one really paid me any mind. They didn't care Raine Edwards was in their midst. They went about their lives as though I didn't exist, which suited me fine. Coxwright Manor was crawling with students from every affiliation. Drinking. Dancing. Dry humping. Actual humping.

But no sign of freaking Dante Wolfe.

And my search was halted in the most annoying way possible.

West shoved me against the wall, and I glared at him. I knew there was only so much he'd do in front of everyone. Knowing that Dante must be here somewhere and would undoubtedly be watching, he wasn't going to do more than harass me a little. A harassment I could deal with, only because of the blind assumption that I wouldn't have to deal with anything more.

Relying on Dante Wolfe to help me even without agreeing to his deal. Just another sign of how grand my failure. And it made me suitably angry in the face of West's cockiness.

"Sweetheart…" he purred, his nose trailing over my face.

For a split second, I was thrust further back than the year before. To eighteen, twenty-four months earlier. When I was still that doe-eyed girl with the rose-coloured glasses who'd wanted West to be like this with me. The girl who had seen this as our future. Who had wanted this as our future. Who, for a fraction of a heartbeat, wondered if this could still be our future. Who, for just one moment of absolute leave of my senses, wondered if I didn't still want it. If it wouldn't be easier.

A life with West meant no more revenge. No need for

Dante's help. No owing the Lord of the goddamned Immortals his three fucking wishes.

Then, West was continuing, and my moment of madness passed. As his hand slid up my side, he said, "Living out a fantasy, Raine? But yours…or mine?"

I looked him over, pouring as much boredom into my tone as possible. "Why doesn't it surprise me that your fantasy is killing me on my wedding day and then me returning from the dead to eek my revenge on you?"

West's smirk was soft as he looked me over. "*Our* wedding day, Raine. Please."

As I looked into those deep blue eyes, I actually believed he was thinking it. He was picturing our wedding. He'd also not disagreed with my statement, and I wasn't naïve enough anymore to think he wouldn't marry me just to kill me. It was even something I might consider if it might give me a chance to kill him first.

"I'm not taking any less than five carats, West."

He smirked. "Oh, sweetheart. You deserve ten."

The traitorous heart within in me, that small part of me who'd prefer to pretend the last twelve months hadn't happened, actually dared to flutter over him and I stamped it down. My whole being shut down in the face of the pure fury I then felt at myself. My weakness.

"If I believed you, maybe I would have accepted."

Something sizzled around us. Not between us. Around us. The distinction was real. West was looking at me the way he'd started looking at me the day I'd confronted him in the hallway and suggested that third-class sex was a generous descriptor of his abilities. He was looking at me like maybe he was capable of…

No, not loving me. Never loving me. I was all-but certain

that West Flintlock was the kind of person our world had completely broken. Emotionally. West could rule the school, would rule any boardroom or negotiation he walked into, but he would never know how to love someone if his life literally depended on it.

But he was capable of wanting me. Wanting me with the kind of power that I wanted Dante, that Dante wanted me. That was how West wanted me now. Something so all-consuming and utterly distracting that it was seared into every fibre of his being, even as the hate for feeling it burned through him as well.

I'd been captured by it in Dante. I'd been so totally subsumed by it and him and the fact that he gave me the space to feel something other than everything that threatened to drag me under on a daily basis. One look from Dante had been all it took to rouse my interest and pique my desire.

But I didn't feel that way when West turned such a gaze on me. I didn't completely lose my mind when West's eyes dripped heat and want and need, suggesting that my body was the only thing capable of sating him. I didn't give a shit.

And even though I didn't give a shit, I could still feel it. That knowledge that West was about to kiss me. The same kind of knowledge as when a *moment* was sparking between two interested parties. Only his sparks were bouncing off me, rendered cold and harmless in the face of my indifference.

West leaned towards me, his lips aiming directly for mine. He went slow, as though in some hideous mockery of offering me the choice – the chance – to stop him. As if he ever gave anyone a chance to deny him something he wanted.

"I wouldn't do that, West," I said quietly.

His eyes dipped to my lips as he licked his. "No?" he asked, his voice low and obviously intending to be alluring. "You still happy enough with second-rate sex?"

"I'd be happy never being touched again if the alternative was being touched by you," I told him, my tone mimicking the seduction in his. "I'd rather have never lived than feel your hands on me again. I'd rather die than kiss you."

"I can make that happen."

I smirked, no fear in the face of his threats. Not those threats. Not threats my own mind tried on me every second of every day. "Be my guest."

His lips rippled into a snarl as he looked me over. "You will regret this, Raine."

"Regret what, West?" I goaded, my voice sultry and soft.

"Regret this little game you're playing. With me. With *him*."

"I'm not playing a game. With either of you. Though it's amusing how jealous you sound, West. I'm simply doing something I know will piss you off far more than any game."

He growled. "And, what's that?" Interesting he let the jealousy quip slide, and I was starting to wonder if, as far as he was capable, West *was* jealous of whatever he thought was between me and Dante.

"I'm surviving. I survived you and I will continue surviving. I will continue to live my life because you want the opposite." At least until he was dead. "And there's very little you can do about it."

He stepped closer to me and dropped his lips to my ear. "What makes you think I won't ruin you, sweetheart?"

Something was making me bold. Something I told myself had nothing to do with the strength Dante seemed to be imbuing me with. So, I ran my hand over West's very hard cock and gave him the biggest shit-eating grin I could muster. "You won't ruin me until you really get the satisfaction of *ruining* me."

"Are you offering?" West asked, his eyes flashing. I didn't move my hand.

"Offering to remove it for you, sure."

He groaned, low and guttural and full of feral need. "You weren't this sexy last year."

"Maybe you just never really knew me?"

"Maybe not," he admitted, his voice ragged. "Why don't you let me know you now?"

I moved my hand up to his chest and he actually swayed away from me. Something clenched in my chest. "Piss weak try, West."

Humour lit his eyes. "What kind of try do you want, sweetheart?"

"Nothing you'd be capable of, West."

"And your Plutonis is?"

"He's not *my* Plutonis," I bristled, and his amusement grew at my reaction.

"Does he know that?"

"You think *you're* my anything?"

"I'm not owned, Raine. I own. And I own you."

I shoved him away from me. I didn't know if the steps he took backwards were from him not expecting it, or him letting me push him away. And I didn't care. "Not anymore."

He laughed. "Go on, then. Run off to your Plutonis. Tell him the big, bad ex made a move on you. Watch him threaten me and yet, for some reason, make no move on me. Again. Why do you think he's all talk and no bite, sweetheart?"

"Why are you?" I spat back and the humour left West's eyes.

His lips snarled again. "You want me to bite, Raine? You just have to ask."

"Fuck off, West."

He took another step back. "I'd rather watch *you* walk away."

I didn't want to give him the satisfaction, but I less wanted to be around him more than necessary. So, before he changed his mind, I walked away. I didn't have the time to exchange insults with him all night anyway. I looked at the time and saw it was twenty to midnight. I needed to find Dante and I needed to do it fast. I had no doubt that, if I failed to find him before his deadline, he would either straight out refuse to help me or he'd ask me for something far worse than three undisclosed wishes.

But he was still avoiding me. Or at least avoiding me seeing him. Fully intentionally, I'm sure. I had no doubt, he had eyes on me. All the better to make sure I didn't see him. But then, maybe he wasn't and someone else had eyes on me in his stead?

Because I saw Riker first, but the smirk he gave me told me he and Dante were taking this hiding from me seriously. Which was ridiculous. Dante wanted me to agree to his deal – he wanted to hold three wishes over me as much as he wanted me to let him help me – so why in the fuck was he making this harder than it had to be?

Which was a stupid question to ask myself because I knew the answer. I'd only spent like two months making it hard for him to do exactly what I was now asking him to do. It was a mind-fuck on both ends, and I could appreciate that. It wasn't going to stop me being annoyed by Dante giving me a taste of my own medicine, though.

I shouldered my way through the crowd. Riker seemed to be doing his damnedest to keep avoiding me. He kept an eye on me as he strode through the throng of kids. I headed for the same place he was, aiming to meet him at the apex of the triangle. He was clearly hoping to disappear before I made it, but I got there a step behind him and grabbed his arm.

He looked down at it like he couldn't believe anyone actually had the audacity to touch him. "Get your fucking hand off me."

"Where is he?" I demanded.

Riker shook his arm from my hand. "I don't see why it matters to you."

I glared at him, under no delusion that Riker didn't know exactly what ultimatum Dante had served me. As his Bishop *and* his friend. "Where is he, Riker? I need to see him before midnight."

"Cutting it a little close, aren't you? Nice you made time to snuggle with your King."

I frowned at him. "Where is he?"

"Doing better chicks than the little King's sloppy seconds."

I lifted my hand to slap him, then held back. He looked over my hand, then my face, his smirk growing.

"Maybe you're not as stupid as I thought."

I shoved against him, pushing him into the wall behind him and making myself as tall as possible. It was still nothing on his height. "I wish I could say the same, but my parents taught me not to lie. Now, where is he? Or so help your manhood, *Bishop.*"

Something bright lit his eyes. Oh, he still thought I was worth less than the dirt on his boot, but he was also willing to give me a chance to change his mind. I knew I literally only had one chance, though, and I wasn't sure how I wasn't going to fuck it up.

"What is your answer?" he asked me.

"You really want to know before him?"

"You being desperate to see him kind of takes the mystery out of it, princess."

"Then why ask? You want to be the one to tell him he could have got his way and you got *in* his way?" I asked.

Riker seemed to be rethinking the sense in putting me in my place. He must know that Dante would talk to me if I missed the deadline. Me missing the deadline would not stop him from asking me why, or lording it over me, or letting me know what I was missing out on. And Riker knew I would not hesitate to point out why I'd missed the deadline. To tell Dante who had made me miss it. And I wouldn't be mentioning West. I doubted Dante would be lenient towards me, but I also doubted he'd let Riker off for it.

"Where is he?" I asked again.

"Upstairs." His tone was grudging, and I inclined my head.

"Was it so hard to be a decent human being?" I asked, saccharine sweet.

He smirked. "If you think that was decency, you have a lot to learn about humanity."

I bristled that he saw through me so easily. "No. I suppose being driven by fear of what your Lord will do to you can't really be called decent."

He took a step towards me and, despite the fear that shot up my spine, I held my ground. "You will watch how you speak to me, princess."

"You will watch how you speak to *me*, Bishop," I spat back.

I could see in his eyes just how badly he wanted to put me in my place. After a few tense heartbeats, he stepped back and indicated I head upstairs. "Third door to the left."

I had seven minutes. I ran up the stairs and barrelled into the room to find him waiting for me, lounging in a chair as if to wonder where I'd been all night. I took in the bed and the heavy curtains. The fire roaring in the hearth. Then brought my eyes back to him and saw he was standing. Which gave me the perfect vantage to finally see his costume.

Dante was dressed as a…

"You have to be kidding me," I muttered, my eyes rolling.

Dante grinned and gave me a mock-bow. "A knight to serve, *mi principessa*."

"I don't need saving, Dante."

"No? Then you reject my deal?"

My jaw tightened and my fists balled at my sides. "I'm not saying that…" I said slowly.

Dante's grin took on a wicked hue as he stepped towards me. "Let me save you, *nuvola*," he purred. It was less begging and more commanding, and all sexy. My whole body responded.

"I'm not some helpless damsel, Dante. I'm asking for help. Work *with* me. Do the things…I can't. I want to save myself, and I've finally admitted I can't do it alone, but I'm not agreeing to anything if you think you're pulling the strings."

He held up his hands. "You are in charge, *cara*. I'm merely the muscle."

I clenched my jaw together before admitting, "I might need some of your brains, too."

His grin was all predatory and I was starting to see there might be some upsides to a sexy costume. Namely, easier access. "You can have whatever of me you need…" His eyes dropped down my body and painfully slowly back up. "Or want."

He knew what of him I needed…and wanted. Even if I'd been resisting. But he didn't know my resistance wasn't just stubbornness. It wasn't just whatever twisted game we'd been playing. It was still the fear that he would look at me differently if he *really* saw me. Because, no matter how little Dante meant to me, I didn't have a great track record with any of it. With whatever he meant to me or whatever Dante thought I meant to him.

Sex. Love. Lust. Romance.

I couldn't say it had ever gone in my favour before.

The one guy I thought I'd been in love with had put on a good show of feeling the same, but he'd just been using me, only to disfigure and discard me in a moment of boredom. I knew his father was as pissed off as mine about West breaking the merger our union would have brought our families. Though for very different reasons. West's family would have stood to gain a lot of wealth and holdings had we married, which everyone had been hoping for. Including me once.

I'd kissed West more than once and I thought it had been perfectly satisfactory. Proof of physical compatibility. A great precursor to more.

I'd thought West not wanting to touch me was borne out of a mutual respect and taking things slowly, even though I'd wanted him to. Even though I'd been practising by myself plenty and knew *just* what I liked.

And then the first time someone touched me... It wasn't West. Though he'd certainly been in the audience, goading them on.

In the months after, I'd found any random guy willing. Only using enough words to convey interest and confirm theirs. I got the job done without any real bother for niceties. None of them had treated me badly. Comparatively. But neither had any of them been particularly fulfilling experiences.

Then there was Dante.

Dante, whose touch was like fire and ice all at once. Dante

who looked at me the way no one had ever looked at me before. It didn't matter if he was playing me. In many ways, I was playing him. What mattered was the way I felt when I was with him. Strong. Powerful. Sexy. Wanted.

He didn't just want me, he wanted to protect me. To help me protect myself.

With.

Not to.

Together.

Not owned.

And it was very difficult to feel nothing about that, even if what I did feel was horrifically complicated and jumbled to the point that I wasn't really sure what it was. Even if I was too scared to look too closely at it.

Dante watched me like he knew what I was going to say. Like he was hoping I'd clue him into what was currently running through my head. As though he had some inkling of my reticence to give into him. I didn't want to think about that. I didn't want to think about the fact that, if he knew, he was giving me space to work it out, to see if I *could* work it out.

"Well, *principessa*?" Dante purred. "One minute to midnight. What will you choose?"

I drew myself up. "You have a deal, but for three wishes I have a condition of my own."

His eyebrow quirked. "*Che cos'è quello?*"

"I'll let you actually teach me how to use my knife properly."

"Worried or excited about that training montage, Raine?"

I frowned and held my ground. "Deal or no deal, Dante?"

The bell on the steeple clock began to chime midnight and Dante's sinful half-smirk made my insides *and* my outsides do weird things. "Oh, it is most definitely a deal, *nuvola*."

As the clock's last chime faded away, I nodded slowly. "Okay. Good."

"What is your first desire?"

I knew what desire he wanted me to say, and I wasn't going to pass it up entirely, but there were other things that needed ironing out first. "I've spent a year wondering how I'm going to destroy West, and I still have no ideas. I've been sheltered from this part of our world. I know it happens. I know who's usually involved. But I don't know how to plan it."

He inclined his head, seemingly not at all disappointed I hadn't just thrown him back onto the bed. "You and I cannot do it alone, *cara*."

I frowned. "What are you suggesting? I suck off every Immortal and beg for their help, too?"

His smirk smouldered and I felt it shoot straight between my legs. "Selfishly, I would prefer you didn't, but that is your choice. I have a simpler solution."

"And, what's that?"

"I will do everything in my power to help you, but I will also need help. As many Immortals as are willing."

I crossed my arms. "One problem with that plan, Dante."

He inclined his head. "*Infatti*."

"Riker would rather kill me than help me."

"*Si*."

"And without him, I doubt anyone else is going to care about your sudden obsession with what's between my legs."

God, but he was gorgeous. Those golden eyes glowed bright as they roved my body, like he could see everything even right through my costume. "Oh, I'm obsessed with far more than what's between your legs, *nuvola*."

What was between my legs tingled pleasantly, even as I groaned in annoyance. "So, step one is getting Riker on my –

our – side?"

His smile actually blew me away. It was so warm and open and impressed. Proud. Amazed. Actually awed. Just as I'd believed that Vanda had thought me bright and shiny and brilliant, I was starting to believe that was how Dante saw me as well. "You picked up more than you thought, then, *principessa*."

I breathed heavily. "No one is going to like this."

"*Peccato*. You need to earn Riker's trust. Once you do, he is harmless."

I raised my eyebrow at him. "You think Riker will ever be harmless to me?"

Dante's tongue swept over his bottom lip as his eyes looked over me. "I think he would have a very hard time hurting you when you owe me three wishes."

"Thinking about cashing them in now?" I tried.

He shook his head as he walked towards me. "*No, cara*. I would rather know what wishes you have right now. What can I do…to you?"

The implied 'what will you *let* me do to you' was evident in the jagged need filling his tone. He was not afraid of begging me. Of pleading with me. Of showing me a vulnerability about what he wanted and hoping I felt the same. Well, lucky for him, when it came to this, I did feel the same.

"You can make me forget I'm about to go to war with your Bishop," I told him dryly.

He grinned. "Your wish is my command."

He pulled me into his arms and kissed me hard. My arms wound around his shoulders and his went around my waist. In his kiss, I felt his gratitude. But what he had to be thankful for I didn't know. I was the one who owed him. It was me who should be thanking him. So, I thanked him the only way I knew how, in the only currency I knew anymore. Not quite sex, but neither of us left unsatisfied.

I had been West's pawn, but I was done letting fear and old habits rule me. Dante was no knight, but I would let him help me. Help me bring down the King. Help me get my revenge. Even if I – we – had to take the Bishop first to get it.

THE END

The Immortals of Lionswood

If you liked *Pawn takes Knight*, share the love and let me know! There are five more instalments to come, including the prequel story. You can also get the safe for work paperbacks from my website.

Gods & Angels

If you liked *Pawn takes Knight*, you might also enjoy *Gods & Angels*. A New Adult darker, high school, bully romance. Book 3 is out soon! Get it here: https://books2read.com/u/38yaGw

From Elizabeth Stevens, writing as E.J. Knox, comes…
A ruthless god. A sinful angel. And the princess between them.

My life is perfect. My life is planned. My life isn't mine.
Promised to a man I love. A man I hate. Not even a man. A god.
Apollo Callahan is that and much more.

My life is broken. My life is fractured. My life isn't free.
Craving a man I hate. A man I need. Not even a man. An angel.
Valen Kincaid is nothing I could ever want.

Though the Saints rule the hallowed halls of Saint Benedict's College, they're anything but saintly. Behind closed doors, they call themselves the Sinners. Sex. Fast Cars. Drugs. Money. The odd assassination or two. Nothing is beneath them, except the next in a long line of women. Can one little princess, searching to break free from her prison tower, bring these mighty lords crashing to their knees?

The stunning first book in the Sinners of Saint Benedicts series.

Prince Of Thorns

If you liked *Pawn takes Knight*, you might also enjoy *Prince of Thorns*. A New Adult darker, enemies-to-lovers, academy, gang romance. Get it here: https://books2read.com/u/bryaD7

From Elizabeth Stevens, writing as E.J. Knox, comes…

The bad boy willing to risk everything – even his life – to get the girl.

People call them the V.I.C.E.S. because they'll wring you for everything you are and leave you ruined. They are the Princes of Rosewood Hall, and no one says no to them. Until now.

Vaughn Saint. The racer. He dubbed the Prince of Thorns. Pretty as a rose, but one touch and he'll leave you bleeding.

He chases death on two wheels at least twice a week. Used to controlling powerful things between his thighs, nothing is more powerful than the lure of the pleasures he promises.

And he wants to give them all to me. Only problem? I'm the daughter of the leader of the Blood Roses. His leader. I'm off-limits. Dad wants me to walk away from all that, not get dragged down deeper into their hell, but Vaughn Saint threatens to take me to the very depths and still have me begging for more. Loving me will kill him.

Not loving me will destroy the both of us.

Pawn takes Knight

Thank you so much for reading this story! Word of mouth is super valuable to authors. So, if you have a few moments to rate/review Raine's story – or, even just pass it on to a friend – I would be really appreciative.

Have you looked for my books in store, or at your local or school library and can't find them? Just let your friendly staff member or librarian know that they can order copies directly from LightningSource/Ingram.

If you want to keep up to date with my new releases, rambles and writing progress, sign up to my newsletter at https://landing.mailerlite.com/webforms/landing/y1n6q2.

Follow me:

Thanks

Oh, the thanks. You know, the more books I write and the faster I write one, the more difficult it gets to do the thanks without sounding like a broken record. So, here I go, being a bit of a broken record.

Thank you to my family for loving me and my weirdness and, as always, my terrible time management skills.

Thank you to my fantastic PhD cohort – talking writing and Romance studies and just life in general with you all means so very much and I'm so glad I've found each and every one of you.

To the beta team – new and veteran – for helping with this one. I was so worried it was HORRIBLE but you guys got me through again ☺

And a final thanks to Charny, who constantly drops everything to read my stuff when I get paranoid and you affectionately, virtually smack some sense into me.

My Books

While you wait for the next release, you can find where to buy all my books in print and eBook at the website; www.elizabethstevens.com.au/ej-knox.

About the Author

E.J. Knox is the Darker/Bully Romance penname of Elizabeth Stevens. E.J. is the name to read if you want darker/bully romance in the Mature YA/NA crossover space. Think high school, college, and academy. E.J. brings my usual wit, banter, and repartee in good old enemies-to-lovers showdowns between alpha males and the sassy heroines strong enough to knock them down a peg or two. There'll be fake-dating, love triangles, kidnapping and danger, second chances, and more.

Writer. Reader. Perpetual student. Nerd.

Born in New Zealand to a Brit and an Australian, I am a writer with a passion for all things storytelling. I love reading, writing, TV and movies, gaming, and spending time with family and friends. I am an avid fan of British comedy, superheroes, and SuperWhoLock. I have too many favourite books, but I fell in love with reading after Isobelle Carmody's *Obernewtyn*. I am obsessed with all things mythological – my current focus being old-style Irish faeries. I live in Adelaide (South Australia) with my long-suffering husband, delirious dog, mad cat, two chickens, and a lazy turtle.

Contact me:

Email: ejknox@elizabethstevens.com.au
Website: www.elizabethstevens.com.au/ej-knox
Twitter: www.twitter.com/writer_iz
Instagram: www.instagram.com/writeriz
Facebook: https://www.facebook.com/elizabethstevens88/